Your Favorite Band Cannot Save You

YOUR FAVORITE BAND CANNOT SAVE YOU

SCOTTO MOORE

A TOM DOHERTY ASSOCIATES BOOK

NEW YORK

YOUR FAVORITE BAND CANNOT SAVE YOU

Copyright © 2016 by Scott Alan Moore

First published in 2016 by Scotto Moore

Cover photo by Shutterstock.com

Edited by Lee Harris

A Tor.com Book
Published by Tom Doherty Associates
175 Fifth Avenue
New York, NY 10010

www.tor.com

Tor® is a registered trademark of
Macmillan Publishing Group, LLC.

ISBN 978-1-250-31489-5 (ebook)
ISBN 978-1-250-31490-1 (trade paperback)

First Tor.com Edition: February 2019

for Jen Moon

Track 01

I was home alone on a Saturday night when I experienced the most beautiful piece of music I had ever heard in my life.

Took me hours to even begin to understand what had happened, actually.

Time stopped while I was listening to it. Elation swept through me, as if I could die now, secure in the knowledge that I had at long last heard the most beautiful piece of music in the world and if I never heard any other music ever again, it wouldn't matter, because all music after this was going to sound like shit anyway.

And then came the secondary realization that I had been listening to this song on repeat for an indeterminate period of time and didn't plan to stop, really, because it was just so good that nothing else mattered. Sometimes you overplay a song and then you burn it out and you don't need to hear it again and you're back to looking for something good like that one used to be, but with this song, you could just keep listening to it forever and your brain would tailor itself to the presence of this song until you literally couldn't live without it. I could feel parts of my personality dissolving, replaced by themes contained within this music.

And then a part of me realized that I desperately needed to use the bathroom, and I had a crisis of faith.

For the first time in hours, I actually tried to take an intellectual action distinct from listening to the music, and a distant part of me noticed how difficult it was, because the music was all-encompassing. I thought to myself, maybe I shouldn't immediately start the song over this time, maybe I could pause it just this once so I could stumble to the bathroom. And in the break, after I had finally paused the music, the silence was a deafening, almost maddening roar in my ears. Like the roar of too many decibels at close range. Like cauterizing auditory nerves with lasers. I don't know, maybe not like that, but it sucked is my point.

And while the music was stopped, I took a look around the room. It had been Saturday night; now daylight was coming in the windows. I was covered in sweat. I was starving. I was exhausted. Some other feeling, too—oh right, panic, which was just getting started. I stood up, wobbly with that "only one foot on the planet" feeling that sometimes comes from too much ketamine on the dance floor, and I hobbled my way down the hallway to the bathroom. I leaned against the wall nearly the entire way until my strength finally reasserted itself. I considered a shower; I thought the sensory stimulus of water pounding on my bare skin might help me regain my composure.

But in the end, the mystery of that incredible music was much more pressing than any other sensory stimulus. When I was finished in the bathroom, I staggered slowly back to my bedroom and sat back down at my desk. My eyes focused on my laptop screen, and I started to piece together what had happened.

· · ·

It started with a Google News alert on the keywords "Surrealist Sound System," which was a band from Madison, where I went to college. This band released several records while I was in school and then broke up; perhaps once every few years since then, I'll learn about a new side project by one of the band members thanks to this news alert. As far as I can tell, very few human beings who did not live near Madison while the band was active have ever heard of this band. Believe me, I've looked—if you Google this band, the top hit is my own blog post lamenting the band's demise, followed by the rest of the internet not giving a shit. They were a flash in the pan in the early web era, so they don't even have a zombie My-

Space page floating around.

This alert led me to a Bandcamp page for a band I'd never heard of called Beautiful Remorse. Bandcamp lets artists set up their own little microsites to sell their music or give it away if they want; as a music blogger, I go there all the time to check stuff out. Beautiful Remorse tripped my news alert because they claimed their music is "for fans of Ganja Lightwagon, The Alkaloids, and Surrealist Sound System." They'd posted exactly one track, a four-and-a-half-minute tune helpfully named "Overture." I was both excited and skeptical—quite a strange claim, to compare your music to a local band that broke up fifteen years ago. Was this a side project I hadn't heard about? Did these people just happen to have (like me, of course) preposterously good taste in underground eclectic music? I immediately paused the previous album I'd been auditioning in order to stream "Overture" from Bandcamp.

Four and a half minutes passed by in a rush. It was like I took a deep breath as the first notes of the track hit me, and exhaled right as the track ended. Both thrilled and deeply frustrated by the experience, I downloaded the track (offered as a freebie), and put it on repeat.

. . .

But then it was Sunday morning, very early, and as the sound of "Overture" receded into memory during my arduous trip to and from the bathroom, my brain informed me that silence would be good for a while, because I very much needed to be able to think clearly.

I was beginning to want more information about "Overture." That's my thing—I've been a music blogger since the earliest days of music blogging, and I'm never satisfied until I've digested not just the music itself, but all available metadata about the music. I need to place it in the firmament, understand where it came from, how it connects to the vast musical genre tree that defines consciousness as we know it. And this was no ordinary track, obviously, no simple confection—it swallowed you up like a drop of rain landing in the ocean and losing its coherence, its own identity.

The Bandcamp page for Beautiful Remorse was maddeningly austere: no liner notes about the band, no copyright information or label affiliation, a bland and abstract swash of colors for an album image, no further information beyond the "for fans of . . ." line and several genre tags that I found to be laughably inadequate and contradictory: "experimental ambient," "baroque metal," "overdubstep," "sounds of nature."

Worse than that: Beautiful Remorse maintained no other presence on the internet beyond its Bandcamp page. No interviews, no photos, no fan forums, no tour listings. No Soundcloud, no Spotify, no YouTube. I searched the Gmail account for my music blog, where hundreds of messages arrive each day from artists, promoters, publicists, and record labels, but no one claiming to represent Beautiful Remorse had ever bothered to contact me. I jumped onto Hype Machine, an aggregator of music feeds from all over the world and a great place to see what other music bloggers are talking about, but no one had ever posted about Beautiful Remorse.

I cracked open the MP3 itself to check the ID3 metadata. Sometimes bands will accidentally leave a paper trail in their early promo tracks, and you'll see comments from the recording engineer about the mix or alternate album art or something like that.

Track: 01
Title: Overture
Artist: Beautiful Remorse
Album: I Shall Not Get Caught a Second Time
Comments: Track 01 of a 10-track album. Check back daily for the next track!

Daily? If their Bandcamp site went up yesterday, triggering my news alert, then I was going to get another track today! This was worth canceling today's plans (which at any rate involved staying at home and being antisocial).

However, there was definitely one thing I could do while I waited. No point keeping this music a secret. I jumped onto Tumblr and prepared to post "Overture," quietly giggling that I would be the first to notify the blogosphere about this insanely good new track, certain that fortune had smiled upon me by alerting me to the existence of Beautiful Remorse. The only challenge: trying to describe "Overture" in words, trying to identify the genres that "Overture" at once mastered and transformed into something new, something far beyond what anyone expected any form of popular music could accomplish.

I decided, as I often do, to coin a new genre name for this music and let my readers fend for themselves. I called it *allurebient* and published the post.

Track 02

After a brief nap, I hopped onto Maxnet, hoping to brag about my latest musical discovery.

Maxnet is a darknet operated by Maxstacy, granddaddy of music blogging. Maxstacy was the first person to publish an MP3 on a blog and say, "Hey, check this shit out!" (He was more articulate than that, but you can look it up yourself if you want a history lesson.) Music blogging soon exploded but he was there first, and in a flash of inspiration, Maxstacy created Maxnet: an invitation-only darknet solely for music bloggers, for those Maxstacy deemed to be the cream of the crop. I've always felt like I lucked into my invitation; when music blogging was in its earliest days, I happened to post about Maxstacy's favorite pop band before anyone else (but him, of course), and my golden ticket to Maxnet was the result. He rarely hangs out on Maxnet anymore, of course; now he's actually working for a major label as a talent-spotter, but he's still blogging and he keeps Maxnet alive to ensure that his elite brand halo among the rest of us lesser bloggers never fades.

I hopped into the central video chat room and took a

look around—Sunday afternoons were always slow, but I saw a few familiar faces pop up. Mocha in Mexico City, Ricochet in Baltimore, William in Austin. I waited patiently for a few moments, and then Imogen Sweetness popped online from New Orleans. She has a script that lets her know when I join and she must have had some free time so here she is. Imogen Sweetness and I have the kind of perfect internet flirtation that comes from knowing I will never leave Portland and she would never agree to meet me in person if I did. I don't know, it works for me.

"Where did you find that track?" she exclaimed immediately. "That is some seriously sick shit."

"Just doing my part to enlighten the kids," I responded with genuine faux modesty.

"Their second track is even more amazing," she continued.

Second track? Shit—was I suddenly an amateur? I refreshed the Bandcamp page for Beautiful Remorse, and there it was: a new, six-minute track entitled "The Awakening." My heart started pounding in anticipation. I popped over to Hype Machine and learned that "The Awakening" had already been posted by about fifty different blogs. Imogen Sweetness posted it first. Which is a little weird. Every music blogger has a different beat; my beat is completely eclectic, so this music makes sense on my blog. But Imogen mostly posts J-pop and obscure '80s covers. Mocha has a deep fascination with Americana and twang, but she posted both "Overture" and "The Awakening," one right after the other. Seemed like Beautiful Remorse was that rare kind of band that truly transcends tight genre definitions.

Ricochet chimed in, "Sounds like ass to me."

I wasn't surprised that Ricochet was not jumping on the bandwagon. I'm not even sure he actually likes music. His blog covers a genre he calls "inverted retro": he believes that there are bands making music that is so terrible that they must be doing it as some kind of practical joke on the music industry. Each of his posts attempts to prove that a given band or artist *must know* how terrible their music is because no sane artist would otherwise make music that bad. And he believes that the only reason these bands have fans is because they're all engaged in some kind of weird performance art to see just how much torture a person is willing to endure in the name of music. It's actually pretty funny when his targets try to defend themselves in his comment threads, since *of course* anyone making "inverted retro" music would deny it by definition.

"Correction," Ricochet said, "it sounds like cats undergoing explosive decompression, in slow motion. But with a singer."

A singer! I could contain my curiosity no longer. I

muted the video chat and pressed play on "The Awakening."

A gorgeous voice filled my ears and a warm ecstatic rush overwhelmed me. My mind filled with visions of swirling stars and lattices of energy. I tried to concentrate on the vocals—she was singing in a made-up language, but I still felt like I could understand her. Not that I could translate her meaning exactly, but somehow I knew she was transmitting and I was receiving. Six minutes rushed by in a heartbeat.

I wiped the sweat off my face and opened my eyes. It took me several minutes before my eyes could focus on my laptop screen. Imogen was actually waving at me, trying to get my attention, and I saw multiple private chat requests from her had piled up. I connected privately, unmuted, and said, "Hey."

"What the fuck kind of modern dance was that?" she asked. "You shouldn't pull that shit on camera—Ricochet says he's going to put the capture up on YouTube, but set it to bad Bolivian psytrance."

Before I could cleverly respond with "There's *good* Bolivian psytrance?" Imogen said, "Let me show you."

Playback began in her window—it was me, from six minutes ago, starting to listen to "The Awakening." The video chat software had caught my reaction, which Imogen (and Ricochet apparently) had started recording. I watched a smile spread across my recorded face and then suddenly I was squirming around and flailing in my chair, laughing out loud and then shrieking with delight, eyes squeezed tightly shut, until the song ended and I regained some semblance of awareness.

I rubbed my face repeatedly, trying to stave off the urge to listen to the track again. Something about that singer's voice—I felt like I recognized it. I felt like I needed to hear it again to be sure. I felt like I needed to hear it again regardless. A lot.

"That reaction . . . it's not normal," I said.

"Not exactly, no."

"Did it happen to you?"

"I don't know. Maybe. Mocha said she fell out of her chair when she heard it the first time."

"Shouldn't we tell someone?" I asked wearily.

"We are in fact telling people. We're telling *thousands* of people on our blogs. Well, in your case dozens, but still."

"It's more than dozens, and I have the easily hacked JavaScript hit counter to prove it."

Then a flash of inspiration struck. In hindsight, this inspiration could be traced back to the original invention of sequential storytelling, but to me, in that moment, it felt like pure genius was flowing through my veins.

"These two tracks are part of an album," I said. "They

are intended to be heard back to back."

Imogen's eyes lit up. "Pipe the audio through your chat client and we can listen together."

You would be correct to ask yourself why the two of us would knowingly repeat a listening experiment that had previously caused documented spasms and collapses. Totally legit question—for someone who hasn't heard this music. It's like asking a junkie if she wants more smack right after watching her girlfriend OD. The answer, sadly, is always yes.

A familiar warm rush swept up over me as the music started up, but the difference this time was I was also hearing Imogen's voice in my headphones at the same time. "Overture" had no vocals, so instead I was hearing Imogen moaning softly, and maybe I was moaning too. Our eyes were locked on each other—well, on each other's chat windows, anyway. Her chat window was maximized on my screen, and for a few moments I thought I could just reach through that window and caress her face, absorb her skin into mine—and then "The Awakening" began, and Imogen and I fell immediately silent.

Because Beautiful Remorse had a singer, and her voice was glorious and immense. Her voice lit up a circuit between Imogen and me. An unstoppable flow of psychic information passed between us. I *knew* Imogen and what she felt and who she was, and because I knew these things about her, I knew she also knew these things about me. And I began to be terrified, and I knew she was too.

Then the song was over. I was breathless, covered in sweat, shivering with fear. Imogen looked flushed, like the color saturation on my screen had suddenly red-shifted.

"God, I feel so stupid," she said. "I had no idea."

"Is that cool?" I asked.

"I mean, sure. Of course it is. Why wouldn't it be?"

"I'm just—I'm still figuring it out myself."

"That's totally cool," she said, and it wasn't awkward at all.

"You sure?"

"Yeah, I just—sometimes living clear across the country from you is not my favorite thing."

"I know the feeling," I said, which wasn't a giant cliché at all. "Listen, you wanna hear those tracks again?" I was asking a question, but I was already starting the music.

Track 03

I knew a product manager at Bandcamp. Not in person or anything, but we got to be email buddies after I became one of the first bloggers in the world to start paying attention to his site. His name or handle or whatever was Carlos at Bandcamp dot com, and after the first few times I linked to some new band on his site, Carlos at Bandcamp dot com emailed me to say thanks and would I help him test some new embed code, which got me onto a private chat channel for Bandcamp employees, just for the duration of the project. But by the time the project was over, I was one of the gang and they never kicked me out.

I jumped online that Monday morning, exhausted and exhilarated after the weekend's adventures, saw the random chitchatty chitchat of a bunch of developers and music nerds, and could barely comprehend how mundane everything seemed in light of the absolute lightning this company had on its unwitting hands. Carlos at Bandcamp dot com was usually late for work and today was no exception, so I had time to kill.

I pinged the whole channel hi and said, "Hey, you guys

must have all heard Beautiful Remorse by now, yeah?"

This was a running joke between the gang and me. Even though they all worked for a hot little music service, they still relied on their pet blogger to point them at the good stuff on their own site.

"Missed that one," said Charlie, QA manager. "Is that filed under NONE MORE GOTH?"

"My boyfriend skipped work this morning to stay home and wait for track three," said Lisa, ecommerce developer.

"So you heard tracks one and two?" I asked.

"Uh, no, he wouldn't take his headphones off when I saw him last night, so I went home."

Carlos at Bandcamp dot com finally arrived on the channel at the leisurely hour of eleven in the morning, and he quickly pinged me in a private chat.

"How do you do it?" he said. "Beautiful Remorse has had an account with us for like seventy-two hours, and they nearly crashed our entire site last night. And some asshole in marketing is already flipping me shit because he can't find *allurebient* in the genre tree."

"Who the fuck are they?" I asked, desperately trying to disguise my pleading impatience behind a veneer of pleading impatience.

"How should I know? You're the hot-shit music blogger, aren't you?"

"They came out of nowhere. They have no discoverable online presence except with you guys."

"Interesting. I should let our PR team know."

"Sure, but first you should find out who they are and tell me. Off the record, of course."

"What are you talking about?"

"I want a name, my friend. I want you to look up their account information and tell me who's uploading that music."

"Uh, sure, first just let me print out our privacy policy and wipe my ass with it in our general counsel's office."

"While you're at it, be sure to let your IT department know that you've been sharing your VPN access with me for years."

I will abbreviate our subsequent polite jocularity, which was summarily interrupted when Bhargava, content management supervisor, announced on the public channel, "Looks like Beautiful Remorse just dropped track three."

Frantically I flipped into the browser tab where the Beautiful Remorse artist page remained open, beckoning me to untold future delights. But after stabbing the keyboard repeatedly to refresh the page, track three did not appear. Then I remembered—actual employees could hit an internal beta version of the site where content was frequently staged on its way to being published. The same system that let bands preview their tracks before they went live allowed employees to preview those tracks if they were paying attention. I flipped to the beta environment and found track three: "Undeniable Presence." I almost kicked off playback immediately, but then a sudden thought jolted me—how could I listen to this track for the first time without Imogen?

I flipped over to Maxnet looking for her. Her autoresponder said, "Be right back, I'm at the beauty salon!" which usually meant she was on her back porch, smoking weed, ignoring the rest of the world with a religious dedication until she felt she was sufficiently baked to go back to operating a keyboard. I could text her. She'd told me I could always text her. I had her number. I could totally text her.

I decided not to text her. I could wait for her to get back online before I listened to this track.

But the gang on the Bandcamp channel didn't wait. The channel got very, very silent for many minutes. Only Carlos at Bandcamp dot com remained active—he hadn't listened to any of the tracks yet, and he was bewildered watching the behavior of everyone around him in their office.

"Shit's getting very weird over here," he said.

"This band is putting out very weird music," I replied.

"Fuck that. I am sticking with Foghat." Carlos at Bandcamp dot com never listened to any of the bands on his own service. Carlos at Bandcamp dot com actually kind of hated music.

A few minutes later, he texted me a photo that he'd taken of a screen in their account management system. Clear as day, I now had the username and email address of the person who was uploading tracks for Beautiful Remorse.

William and Mocha saw me active on Maxnet and I got a flurry of questions: "Don't you have Bandcamp access? When is track three coming out? Are you going to share it with us before it's released?"

"I'll share it as soon as Imogen is back online," I said. I could hear them rolling their eyes through their respective keyboards.

"You guys sound like you're in a cult," said Ricochet.

"Uh-huh. And what are you listening to this fine day?" I asked.

"Rhino just put out a box set—*Best of Swedish Hair Metal from 1982, the Remixes.*" He was serious too.

"Hey, you guys know any promoters or label reps named Airee Macpherson?" I asked, passing on the name I'd learned via Carlos at Bandcamp dot com. I hadn't had time to properly Google her.

"Airee Macpherson is a singer, not a promoter," said William. "She lives in Austin."

"You've heard of her?"

"Pretty sure my entire last comment indicates that I've heard of her, hot shot."

You could find Airee Macpherson on the internet. Not her band, Beautiful Remorse—at least, not outside of Bandcamp. But Airee had her own Tumblr, a collection of sarcastic images and what I assumed to be journal excerpts and cryptic quotations. Anyway—you know how sometimes a person's online presence is so immediate and so distinct that you feel like you know exactly what that person looks like, even if they haven't posted a single selfie? I had that experience—Airee Macpherson popped into my mind, fully formed, and holy god she was beautiful.

"Nothing holy," she whispered. I screamed a little.

Imogen finally jumped online as I regained my composure—I wanted to say "my sanity" but let's be clear, my sanity was in question on some level before any of this ever happened. She read back through the past half hour, then private messaged me: "You have early access to track three? You should have texted me!!"

I never text her. I've never texted her. I should have texted her. I didn't text her. Anyway.

On the public channel, I said, "Track three incoming. Take a moment to prepare and then I'll pipe the audio through the channel."

"Thanks for the heads up," Ricochet said. "I'll be keeping you all on mute, in what I hope you interpret as indignant rage despite my known penchant for severe apathy."

"This track is called 'Undeniable Presence,'" I said. My hand was trembling as I kicked off playback.

I was obliterated, really. Just sort of crushed into atoms. And then without warning, something gathered me up in a deep, luscious embrace and reassembled me. I could feel it—I could feel *her* consoling me, sweeping away the emptiness, signaling the absolute fact of something greater than both of us just out of sight.

Imogen felt it too. And I could feel Imogen having the same realization as me—that the woman singing, Airee Macpherson, was the nexus of something remarkable and potent, something deeply soulful and magnetic, something anyone would desperately crave once they realized it was within reach.

The song was over much too quickly. Track two, "The Awakening," had been a luxurious six minutes. Track three, "Undeniable Presence," required only two and a half minutes to sear its mark into us. It took me a moment to clear my head. I checked the channel and no one was saying anything. I messaged Imogen but she wasn't saying anything either.

I flipped back over to Airee Macpherson's Tumblr, and without hesitation, I messaged her.

Your album is completely out of control. I write for a music site called Much Preferred Customers. Can I interview you?

By the time I got back from the fridge with a soda, she had already responded:

Yeah I heard of you. Been waiting for you to get in touch. We have a show tomorrow night in Austin. Can you make it?

Track 04

My sheltered Portland skin was unaccustomed to the blazing orb of death that reigned over Austin when I arrived the next day. William from Maxnet met me at the airport. He was the first person from Maxnet I'd actually physically met, and we couldn't decide if we should awkwardly hug or just kind of do that hipster standoffish nod-and-be-cool thing. Hugging seemed weird just on principle but he was letting me stay with him tonight so being standoffish seemed weird too. Finally we did one of those almost-air-hugs, where there was definitely physical contact but kind of like how your grandma hugs you where it's really just kind of patting you gently to say, "That's nice, kid, now get me a fucking Marlboro and get the fuck out of my way."

"How'd you hear about this show?" William asked. "I checked the listings for Emo's and it's supposedly some tribute band tonight."

"I scored an interview," I said, almost sheepishly. William looked at me like I had just announced I was here to bomb the Capitol Building. Bloggers at my level score promos all the time, but we rarely score interviews.

We made small talk in his car as we headed into the city. He was a very genial guy, and naturally curious how I could drop everything and fly to Austin on a day's notice, since for most people, music blogging doesn't pay the bills. Doesn't even pay bill, singular. I'm a visual designer who picks up gigs a few times a year that pay bank, and then I sit on my ass the rest of the year and do whatever. Similarly, I was curious what line of work allowed him to cut out in the middle of the day to pick me up in his swank luxury BMW equipped with fancy Harman Kardon car stereo. Turns out—coder. The subject sufficiently exhausted, we lapsed into a brief silence.

But we are music bloggers, and we do not abide silence.

William's iPhone and his car stereo made sweet Bluetooth love, and suddenly music emerged. William's beat was very specific: he was into minor exotica that only existed on original vinyl and was never reissued in any other format. So think of Esquivel, Martin Denny, or Les Baxter—and now imagine the glorious unexplored world of artists who weren't as good as those guys, but also with vinyl pops and scratches faithfully preserved, delivered with highest sonic reproduction via high-end car stereo equipment. If you were to guess that he was baiting me, you'd be partially right; a polite man in his seat would have offered me a chance to put on a playlist, which I would have politely declined because he was after all the driver, which he could have politely declined because I was a visiting dignitary from Maxnet, and we could have been listening to decent fucking music at that point, so on that level, he was definitely baiting me. But then his own actual choice of music—wait, did I say "partially"? Because yeah that was 100 percent baiting me.

"Dare I ask what we're listening to?" I dared to ask.

"Japanese vibraphone covers of Beach Boys deep cuts," he replied.

"Interesting. The Beach Boys tunes I'm familiar with typically have melodies."

"They're definitely using a weird tuning system on this record."

He delivered me to the front door of Emo's with almost an hour to spare before my interview, and promised to be back for the show later that night. As his BMW rocketed off into the distance, I stood quietly on the nearly empty street, gaping at my surroundings. I had perhaps imagined some fancy tour bus would be parked out front with a glorious Beautiful Remorse logo in electric paint across the side. Instead, there was a van and a scooter parked nearby, and either vehicle could have belonged to anybody on the block. I checked on my phone—track four had not been released yet for some reason. I pulled out my headphones, and with immense self-control, did not play any of the other three Beautiful Remorse tracks, fearing the idea of having a seizure on the street more than I longed to hear the music again. But my eyes immediately began scanning down the street, and into the nearby alley. Maybe, I frantically schemed, I could find a park bench to lie down on, or an open-bed pickup truck I could climb into—

"Much Preferred Customers?" someone said from the doorway of Emo's.

I spun and saw a waifish young woman with short, bright red hair peering down at me from the entrance. She wore a tank top with a screen print of Joan Jett in a tracksuit from her Runaways days. I immediately recognized her: Sierra Nelson, former drummer for Surrealist Sound System. I'd seen her and her old band play approximately infinity times back in Madison.

"Thought that was you," she murmured.

"You recognize me?"

"Who else reviewed SSS every week in the *Badger Herald*?"

The answer, of course, was no one. I did that. That was me. She recognized me. Jesus! She must have joined (or formed!) Beautiful Remorse after Surrealist Sound System broke up.

"C'mon, Airee's waiting for you," she said, and she

led me into the venue.

We headed through the auditorium, where several roadies were setting up. Maybe some of them were actual members of the band, given the suspicious manner in which they stared my direction. Or maybe they were staring at me because I was sticking close to their hot drummer Sierra. We didn't stop to chat.

Sierra led me into the dressing room, and without any warning or ceremony, I was suddenly in the same room as Airee Macpherson, the voice of Beautiful Remorse. Sierra closed the door quietly behind me, leaving me alone with Airee.

Was she as gorgeous as my imaginary ideal of her physical perfection that I'd been carrying around in my head? No, because that perfect vision in my head was missing all the little details, all the little flaws that actually make a person real. Honestly she was plain to look at, in the same way I judge myself to be plain when I look in the mirror. Not ugly, not grotesque, but not glamorous, not striking. Plain as in unremarkable, with her hair down loose, wearing a ratty T-shirt and gym shorts.

"You're not what I expected," she said.

"I do hear that sometimes," I replied.

The show was hours from now and she was already assembling the makeup she planned to apply. At first I thought: aha, this is how she will transform into a gorgeous rock star. But then I took a closer look: this wasn't your typical array of beauty cosmetics. This was serious stage makeup: grease paint, facial prosthetics, a handheld airbrush gizmo I'd never seen before. Several masks and wigs nearby made it clear: she intended a serious transformation tonight. She kept puttering with her makeup, selecting and organizing various pencils and brushes, and I just stood there gaping until finally she said, "Sit the fuck down, you're making me nervous."

I found a spot on the couch behind her, where I could see her face in the mirror. She made eye contact with me for the first time, and I suddenly became exceedingly self-conscious.

"You came a long way for an interview. Gonna ask me any questions?"

I was on the spot. Look, music bloggers aren't journalists. We don't get backstage passes on the regular. We definitely don't talk to artists on any kind of frequent basis. I've interviewed a few people in my time, but exclusively by email. I found myself feeling massively unprepared and disappointed in myself for not thinking this all through before I ever got on an airplane to Austin.

"When are you releasing track four?" I finally asked. My voice was unexpectedly dry, like I was about to choke.

"We're recording it live tonight. Dropping it online before midnight is the plan. It's called 'There Will Be Consequences.'"

"Is that . . . I mean, does that actually mean something?"

She cocked her eye at me. "Are you seriously asking me if my shit might actually mean something?" My cheeks burned with stupid embarrassment. "It *all* means something. The song titles mean something. The lyrics mean something. The fucking chord changes mean something." She spun around to look at me directly. "And you being here tonight—*that* means something."

"What's it mean?"

She swiveled back around to her mirror, disenchanted even with scolding me.

"I hate liner notes," she said. "I hate giving away all the mystery. The music speaks for itself."

"Then why do interviews?"

"I don't. This isn't. Get over yourself. Do you even have ten people reading your smug little blog?"

I had a few thousand people reading it, but I knew what she was getting at.

"You're not here to interview me," she continued. "You're here to watch the show. You're an invited guest." She smiled unexpectedly. "Listen, I've got to shower. Hang out in the bar until the show. I'll see you afterward." She expertly shuffled me out of the room before I even realized what she was doing or what she'd just said.

By the time William caught up to me later that night, I'd sussed a few things out. Beautiful Remorse was technically the opening act, scheduled to play from 9:15 to 10 p.m. They had a video crew on hand to capture the set. They did not have a merchandise booth, which left open the question of how they were fronting the money for a video crew without record label backing. For that matter, none of the roadies or other band members would talk to me about where the tour was headed next or why they hadn't bothered to promote this show locally in the first place.

"We promoted the show to the right people," Sierra finally admitted when I caught her heading up to the stage for sound check. "True fans. Aficionados." She probably winked mischievously when she added, "And of course, music bloggers."

"Nobody cares about music bloggers."

"Airee just wanted you to see our first live show. Seriously—check the Hype Machine. You were the first blogger to write about us. She didn't get it at first, but . . . I convinced her you knew your shit. Cuz I remembered what you said about SSS back in Madison. God, couldn't forget that kind of praise, not when you're a dirt-poor little brat trying to learn the drums in front of two hundred people every week for three years. Totally kept me going, you know that?"

She was thanking me for supporting her before either one of us understood the stakes involved in giving a shit about music. I mean, you don't *have* to care at all about music, there's no stakes involved in basically flitting through life without a favorite song or a favorite band, people do it all the time and lead full, satisfying lives and their funerals are well-attended by sad people. But if you *do* decide to care about music—and in Sierra's case, if you decide to care so much that you have to *play* music—then your whole life is changed. You're always on the hunt for the next best song.

"Sierra," I said, when I thought I had her full attention, "tell me what's really going on here."

To my surprise, she took a moment to look around and see if anyone from the crew or the venue was within earshot, and when she was satisfied no one could hear her, she said, "The album we're releasing is a musical incantation. It draws power virally from the psychic network of minds that are rapidly attuning their brain waves to our musical signature. You must have already felt how you can't ever shake hearing one of our songs in your mind, even when you're listening to some other stupid song on the radio or whatever. It's charging you up like a battery, and every time we release a new track, we're charging the entire network up to a new energetic level.

Tonight's gonna be special, though, because it's our first live performance. Our first chance to charge and draw directly from a raw physical network of minds. Airee's got something big planned if she can pull enough power from her collective audience. Does that answer your question?"

"Are you joking? No, that doesn't answer my question. What's going to happen here tonight?"

"We're gonna play a fucking gig," she said.

When the doors opened, William and I made our way to a position front and center, leaning against the barrier in front of the stage. No one except the occasional bouncer patrolling in front of us was going to get between me and Airee Macpherson tonight.

William had brought foam earplugs with him to offer to young women in the crowd as a conversation starter. I had my own high-end pair with me, of course. I felt lucky I'd never suffered hearing loss as a younger idiot attending shows, and now that I was older and wiser, I had zero desire whatsoever to risk losing it tonight or any other night. William gave his own pair away.

The lights dimmed, and the extremely familiar and pleasing opening passages of "Overture" began in the darkness as one by one, the band entered and began taking their places. A huge chill almost overwhelmed me. I realized I'd only ever listened to this densely layered electronic masterpiece on headphones. I'd never heard it blasted out of a professional sound system at maximum safe volume while leaning on a gigantic subwoofer.

Sierra's confident drumming kicked in as the band transitioned from the prerecorded "Overture" into a live version of "The Awakening." I say "version" because it rapidly became clear that they didn't intend to stick to the precise arrangement they used on the recording. The instrumentation was different, for starters: more muscular, not as smooth. The lights rose very slowly on a tight four-piece unit: drums, guitar, bass, keyboards, each with a laptop, pedal station, and sampler. The texture of their sound wasn't as silky as the recording, but their rhythm was absolutely locked. They were each dressed in matching form-fitting black robes that gave them maximum mobility while eliminating most of their physical distinctions. Under these dim blue and purple lights, amidst a light haze from the fog machine, wearing identical wigs and makeup, it was impossible to determine anyone's gender or ethnicity, even standing as close as we were. I wouldn't have recognized Sierra if I hadn't known she was drumming.

My whole body tensed up when I realized "The Awakening" was almost over. I glanced over at William. He was frozen in rapt attention, back arched, swaying slightly, his hands gripping the railing of the barrier in front of him.

Almost in pain, really. The two young women on either side of him seemed a little more nonplused, but William seemed like he was on the verge of something not at all enjoyable.

Then a surprising figure lurched out of the darkness from the back of the stage. Towering over the rest of the band, the figure was draped in diaphanous strips of red, dark red, and darker red. Its arms extended into long bony claws, and its head was an enormous goat skull with gleaming eyes and towering horns. For a split second I thought I was on the set of a terrible prog rock music video, but then the goat creature sang and the room fell impossibly silent.

It must have been Airee Macpherson inside that towering goat-head beast-thing costume, singing the first verse of "Undeniable Presence." And I mean singing the absolute living fuck out of it. My brain kind of shorted out for a minute or two. If you imagine synaesthesia as a blending of senses, you could say I was experiencing a form of synaesthesia in which all the senses were reduced to sonic inputs on some level, and my entire existence was converted into rippling ecstatic audio waveforms—a transformation that felt irreversible, albeit only briefly.

Someone elbowed me hard in the back, almost driving me to my knees. A very large man was pushing his way through the crowd to get to where I was standing. I want to say he was oblivious to me in his pursuit of Airee's voice; I mean, I understood the impulse. But his willingness to throw an elbow at a stranger was probably just barely lurking below the surface of his conscious mind at all times; something in the air tonight gave him permission to act on it. I caught myself on the railing of the barrier on my way down, then spun furiously to face my (hopefully) inadvertent attacker. He glared at me with a comically menacing expression.

William suddenly lurched in between the two of us, got his face right in the other guy's face, did the proper alpha male chest bump to make it clear we owned this particular chunk of floor. I'm not sure why this of all things caught William's attention in the middle of Airee's performance, but I was sincerely glad he'd noticed.

The guy lifted William up off his feet and almost threw him across the floor. Bouncers started shouting and climbing the railing, but Airee's attention was on the guy too.

*"YOU THINK YOU CAN JUST START SOME SHIT AT ONE OF **MY** SHOWS?"* Airee shouted, her voice amplified by bone mics inside her costume goat helmet. ***"THERE WILL BE CONSEQUENCES!"***

That marked the start of the band's next song.

Remember how I had innocently tagged their first track as *allurebient*, hoping to imply "seductively trippy" or some shit? Yeah, so this was as far from seductively trippy as I could imagine. "There Will Be Consequences" was a raw aural assault. Airee's voice was nails across the cosmic chalkboard, amplified to eleven, and the band had seemingly abandoned Western musical chord progressions in favor of feeding their instruments into invisible industrial grinders. Amazingly Sierra was keeping a fierce beat in the middle of it all—you could fucking dance to this shit. A couple of cannons went off on the far sides of the stage, shooting flames into the air and causing the entire crowd to rise up in a roar of glee.

The big guy saw trouble headed his way; he went ahead and tossed William aside like he was a rag doll. Three bouncers pounded into him, surrounding him in a flurry of blows, and suddenly the energy on the floor went nuts.

A mosh pit exploded into existence behind me. I've been in some mean mosh pits before. Not mean as in trying to hurt your feelings or whatever. Mean as in this is some serious shit but look, we are all in it together so let's take care of each other as we slam against each other forcefully and mercilessly in pursuit of bone-crushing nirvana. This mosh pit was different. The people crowd-surfing weren't volunteers. They were being hurled into the air shrieking and passed around like puppets or dolls. Fights broke out over which assholes were manhandling whose girlfriends; which seemingly innocent pixie was actually wielding sharpened fingernails for raking across bare skin; why every now and then some unwilling crowd-surfer was suddenly dropped on their back or their face. The big guy who had thrown William stood up with a roar from underneath a pile of angry people.

Security personnel swarmed from the back of the venue to break things up. I was pinned against the barrier, huddling, trying not to get stomped, trying to avoid being underneath some human missile as it careened toward the floor. I could barely manage a self-preservation instinct in the chaos, let alone the instinct to cushion someone else's fall—probably would just break my bones anyway if I tried. People took advantage of the momentary misdirection of security's attention, and started climbing the barrier in the other direction, aiming to climb the giant towers of loudspeakers on either side of the stage, or worse, aiming for the band.

I had a few spare moments to study their faces—the faces of the possessed, racked in uncontrollable spasms of almost-agony—but security didn't seem to be affected. Neither did I, for that matter, or the petite young women that William had befriended, who were so thin they were actually sliding underneath the barrier to try to get to safety.

This experience lasted about three minutes, at the end of which, someone from the venue pulled the plug on all the electricity to the stage. In the sudden abrupt darkness, before the house lights had a chance to rise, I heard a shriek from above and then a horrible crashing sound, and then silence . . . and then, moans rising up. The house lights finally came up, and one of those towers of loudspeakers was sprawled out on the floor. Toppled, I guess you'd say. I finally found William—his right leg was pinned underneath one of them.

I turned toward the stage. The band was nowhere in sight.

Track 05

I was sleeping in the hospital waiting room when Sierra found me. She roused me roughly and offered me a cup of shitty hospital coffee.

"You look okay," she said. "You okay?"

I had to pause for a genuine think before I answered that question.

"What time is it?" I asked.

"Almost six a.m. C'mon, we're giving you a ride," she said, trying to inspire me to stand up.

I didn't comprehend at first. I thought she meant a ride to the airport, but my flight wasn't until later that afternoon.

"A ride to Houston," she clarified. "That's where we're headed. Next show is tonight."

"You're doing a show tonight?" I asked, trying to disguise my raw incredulity.

She gave me a condescending stare.

"My friend went into surgery about three hours ago," I told her. William's tibia and fibula in his right leg were broken and most of the surrounding ligaments were torn.

They were hooking him up with sufficient metal plating to hold the whole mess together while it healed. He was lucky.

I matched her condescending stare with my own very hard stare.

"I'm surprised the police are letting you leave town," I told her.

"Can't stop us," she said, almost muttering, half shrugging, kind of not admitting what she was admitting.

"Stopping people's actually one of the main things the police are good at," I said.

"Maybe. Not these police."

"And what's so unique about these police?"

"They wanted to see the video from the show."

Oh.

Oh, Jesus, what?

"Yeah, we don't have all day here. Maybe another half hour before the station calms down and someone thinks to wonder what happened. We need to be very gone by then."

"Won't they just come after you?"

"They will definitely go after the tour bus we are sending to Albuquerque. For the big show we're playing tonight in Albuquerque. We took out ads in the newspaper there and everything."

"I thought you were playing in Houston tonight."

"Yes! You're catching on. Now c'mon, the van's outside."

"If you're trying to convince the police you're playing in Albuquerque tonight, how do you expect to pull an audience in Houston?"

"That's what we need *you* for! Will you please pull your shit together and let's *go*?"

I had that one moment right there where I could have just stepped off the roller coaster. I should have stayed to make sure William was going to be all right. I should have clued in that if these people were planning on running from the police, then the last thing I should do is go with them on the lam. I should have recognized how much antipathy was baked into what they were doing.

But then she said, "Airee's gonna let you be the first to hear the next track."

Jesus. Jesus fucking Jesus. I was so entirely *owned* I couldn't stand myself, but I got up, threw my shitty hospital coffee in the trash, and followed her out to the van.

. . .

Sierra sat next to me in the backseat, carefully gazing out the window and feigning disinterest in my conversation with Airee. The driver was the band's bassist, a woman who'd introduced herself to me as Susie Satori.

On the floor behind me, two young women were curled up napping—the guitarist and keyboardist. They were twins, and we were never introduced. Another van followed behind us with the band's gear and two roadies. The video crew had been dismissed to parts unknown to edit the footage. The track from last night, "There Will Be Consequences," was already blowing up in the musical blogosphere, and some of the reports coming in were disturbing. Parties that went south in a hurry; screaming matches about how loud the track should be played; people smashing their stereo equipment; warnings not to listen to it while driving.

The deal was I would get first dibs on posting the new Beautiful Remorse track on Much Preferred Customers. The catch was that I would be introducing it as the debut track from a new band called the Augmented 4th. But I'd be expected to write the post in a wink-wink kind of fashion to make it clear to my loyal followers that yeah, this actually, secretly, was That Band You're All Talking About. They wanted me to jump on Maxnet and quietly spread the word as well, get other bloggers talking about this new band too. And the button on the agreement was: promote the Augmented 4th's debut show tonight in Houston. Get as many of the faithful there as possible.

"They'll listen to you," Airee said, almost nonchalant

about it, "because you're my *Herald*. So that's the deal."

Yeah, I skipped right over that part the first time she said it. Like, I'm going to just pretend you're not giving me an official title, lady.

"If I listen to this new track," I said, "am I going to go crazy like everyone did last night?"

"Not everyone was affected last night," she replied carefully. "You weren't. The bouncers weren't."

Oh—of course. Me and the bouncers—we were wearing earplugs for the show. Mine were industrial grade, meant for construction sites. I wasn't exposed to the full signal of the music.

"Anyway, no, I don't need to repeat myself in my work," she said. Not haughtily—just blandly matter-of-fact about it like any other supernaturally creative mad person might be. She handed me her iPhone and her Ultrasone Signature Pro studio headphones. "If you'd rather not be the first person to hear and post that track, by all means let me know. I'm sure your friend Imogen Sweetness would be thrilled to get the chance. Don't look so surprised—you're not the only one who requested an interview with me." Then she swiveled back around to face the highway from the passenger seat of the van.

I looked down at the iPhone in my hand, which displayed the title of the new track: "You've Been Given a Simple Choice."

I put the headphones on and started the track. It was a ballad. I should have guessed—this album was *due* for a ballad.

· · ·

I jumped onto Maxnet and addressed the entire channel at once.

"Hey people—gather round, I've got a bit of a scoop for y'all."

One by one, I saw avatars light up in the chat room as fellow bloggers switched their focus back to Maxnet from whatever trivial internetting they'd been in the midst of. To my utter surprise, the granddaddy himself, Maxstacy, was one of those who answered the call.

"I surely do hope so," he said in the bland but terrifying manner that I assume every legend maintains.

Strangely, Imogen did not appear. Perhaps egotistically, I thought she'd be excited to hear from me after such a long absence. (An entire day! I know!) I thought about texting her. I almost texted her. I really should have texted her. I did not in fact text her.

"I've got the next track," I said. I didn't have to say the next Beautiful Remorse track. They knew. "I'll give it to anyone on Maxnet who's willing to promote their show tonight." And when general agreement followed, I said,

"There's a catch. They want to be promoted as the Augmented 4th now."

After a small pause, Ricochet chimed in with "AHA-HAHAHAHAHAHAHAHA—no, seriously, are you sure they don't want to be the Artists Formerly Known as Beautiful Remorse? Because *that's* got a ring to it, amirite?"

Of course, Ricochet wasn't wrong to question this weird change of direction. When you build buzz that rapidly, you definitely don't burn it just as rapidly and expect career longevity. But I couldn't explain the true reason Airee was changing the band's name—to keep their tour going as long as possible before bad consequences caught up to us.

Then Maxstacy DM'd me.

I repeat: I received a direct message from the godfather of music blogging, for the first time since I received my invitation to join Maxnet years ago.

"What happened in Austin?" he asked. "Are you even still there?"

Cold sweat—I'd seen a few news reports and blog items about a crowd disturbance and multiple injuries at an Austin rock show, but ironically, the night's headliner was currently taking the blame, even though they hadn't had a chance to perform.

Anticipating my question, he said, "William hasn't

been active since before he left to meet you at Emo's."
Pause.

I was staring at the keyboard of my laptop, connected to Maxnet via hotspot, parked at a truck stop,
alone in the backseat of the van while the band was inside eating at a presumably horrifying truck stop diner.
I was enmeshed in something I didn't understand and
couldn't back out of; I had left William alone in the
hospital without saying good-bye; I was confused
about my own culpability in last night's debacle; I
knew something was weird about my enthusiasm for
carrying out my end of the deal I'd made with Airee;
and now I had the founder of Maxnet asking me
pointed questions about my involvement.

And I didn't care, because I had made a simple choice.
The maddeningly seductive memory of Airee's voice
singing that ballad was all-encompassing. I was making
that same simple choice minute by minute, second by
second, and loving it more and more as time went by. It
was as though each time I remembered it, I was burn-
ing away any resistance I might have to remembering it
again, and the cycle kept repeating like a nested series of
musical spirals unfolding in my mind. Or something.

"William's going to be fine," I said, not entirely certain
how true that was. "He was injured, but not as badly as he
could have been."

A long pause followed, where Maxstacy was either carefully considering what to say next, or he was typing and deleting and typing and deleting to try to get it right, or he was just checking email in another window and forgot about me for a bit. But eventually he said, "How are you holding up?"

Could have been a lot worse than "How are you holding up?" Could have been "What the hell did you do?" or "Should I be calling the police?" but instead it was a seemingly genuine inquiry about my well-being. Which I wasn't prepared to answer, at least not in full.

I said, "I'm fine, I think. But I could really use your help promoting this show."

· · ·

We were an hour away from Houston when I saw Maxstacy's post go up on his site, the very simply and effectively named Maxblog.

"You've Been Given a Simple Choice"
The Augmented 4th
Self-released
Regular readers with keen ears will almost immediately recognize the musical rapids from which the Augmented 4th draws its inspiration. Yet the formal construction of

"You've Been Given a Simple Choice"—superficially, a '70s era soft rock ballad—almost disguises the raw beating heart inherent in the track. Like a certain recent flash-pot band that everyone is talking about, the Augmented 4th relies on the conceit of gibberish lyrics (a trend that most notably includes Sigur Rós and its introduction of "Hopelandish" to the alt-rock lexicon), but let there be no question that the intensity of the song's English title is abundantly apparent in the female singer's powerful, throaty belting. Every guttural phrase that rises out of the austere orchestration is a plea for you—yes, *you*—to make that simple choice, to raise your hand in solidarity with a singer who is clearly desperate for you to join her. On what mad quest, we are not fortunate to know, but her charisma compels you. If you have followed the meteoric rise of a similar band that came out of nowhere recently, you will recognize this vicious yet gorgeous vocal style.

God only knows what that voice must be like in concert.

Conveniently, those of you in the Houston area have a chance to find out TONIGHT. Tickets to the Augmented 4th's surprise show at the Nightingale Room are now on sale, and rumor has it that someone clued in the locals already, so tickets are going fast. But you, my lovely Maxsters, can use the discount code *allurebient* to get half-price tickets online.

Download the track

Buy tickets

• • •

The show sold out with an hour to spare before showtime.

Airee asked me to wait in the van for this show. She said, "I need you to be ready just in case something goes wrong tonight. I don't expect anything to go wrong, but you never know. I didn't expect a riot last night."

"What exactly *did* you expect last night?" I pressed. "Or I mean—what do you expect from this tour?"

"Hard to say," she said. "Worst case, I take over the planet by the time we release track eight. Best case, I open a portal back to my home dimension by track seven and get the fuck out of here instead. It's a little unpredictable. I'm still learning."

I stared at her. I kept staring at her. I stared some more. Lots of staring.

"See, it's this warm feeling of trust that I enjoy most about you," she said. "Look, I know you're upset because the people at the show tonight will get to hear the new track before you. But you still get to premiere the new track online tomorrow."

I said, "Wait, go back to the part about the . . . the dimension, or the . . . you said the portal—" and then I just wound up staring at her again.

She actually put her hands on my shoulders. It was weird and strangely awesome. Like sticking your tongue on a battery and getting a shock, except the charge in this case was her charisma. Also, I wasn't sticking my tongue on her and I'm sorry about that image.

"I am building to something very intense," she said, "and I would prefer that you don't get hurt."

"What about all those other people?"

"I don't have as much of a preference there," she said. "But I do want my *Herald* safe right until the end."

I said, "What do you mean, the end? The end of the tour?"

She just gave me a look. I was half kidding. I wasn't sure I wanted to know what happened after the tour.

I said, "I want the tour to last a long time."

She said, "One track daily and this ain't a double album."

She left me in the front seat of the band's van, parked across the street, waiting for the show to be over, watching roadies smoke on the loading dock of the venue. The line to get in snaked all the way around the block so I got to do some quality people watching even though I was parked behind the building.

Then Sierra appeared briefly on the loading dock,

phone in hand, glancing at the line as though she was looking for someone specific. Apparently she actually was—she waved, and someone waved back and broke out of the line heading for Sierra. Venue security was stationed even on the loading dock, but Sierra had an extra backstage pass to give to—oh.

Sierra handed the backstage pass to Imogen Sweetness, and the two of them disappeared inside the venue together.

Suddenly my very simple choice seemed much more complicated. I mean, I guess it made sense that Imogen was here. New Orleans wasn't that far from Houston. Closer than Portland, obviously. Maybe Imogen scored an interview too. Except Airee doesn't give interviews. So why did Imogen get backstage access when I was stuck out here in the van? What did Airee want with Imogen?

"*Sacrifice,*" Airee whispered in my mind, and I officially freaked the fuck out.

Track 06

I jumped out of the van and bolted across the street, trying to catch Sierra and Imogen before the stage door by the loading dock slammed shut. Not only did I fail to get there in time, but security saw me sprinting in their direction and was extremely ready to knock me onto my ass when I got within range.

"Okay, I deserved that," I muttered. It fucking hurt. I didn't even try to argue with the guy. He was just doing his job, I didn't have a backstage pass for this show, and the roadies on the loading dock wouldn't even make eye contact with me.

My best chance was to hope they still had tickets at the door even though they were sold out online. The line wrapped around the block and they hadn't started letting people in yet. I was too nervous to just stand and wait.

I could text her. I had her number. She gave it to me specifically so that I could text her, someday, if I felt like it. Or call her? Maybe she had wanted me to call her? I couldn't remember why I had her number, actually.

I texted her: "What are you doing here?"

A long pause followed. Then she texted back: "Who is this?"

Because, of course, she didn't have *my* number, because I never gave it to her, and I had never texted her, and I had never called her before.

I said, "It's MPC. How did you get a backstage pass?"

"Interview," she said.

"She doesn't give interviews!"

"She gave you one, didn't she?"

"No, she most definitely did not. What's the deal?"

No response. I waited impatiently. I don't suppose anybody truly waits patiently, but this was pure absurdism. The line finally started moving. I crawled forward before hearing the word passed down: usually a line like this forks into two lines, one for will-call and one for ticket sales. This was all will-call; there were no tickets for sale. My next best chance was to pretend I hadn't heard this, and then get to the front and hope for a miracle.

I dropped out of line. A lot of strange things were happening lately, but expecting friendly, positive miracles was a stretch.

I drifted back toward the van, unable to think clearly. I pulled out my laptop, jumped back onto Maxnet, and scrolled back through the main channel history to see if I'd missed anything important while I was on the road. Sure enough—a debate between Imogen, Mocha, and

Ricochet about whether Imogen had time to make it to the Houston show. She couldn't afford a direct flight, but if she jumped in her housemate's car and took off immediately, she'd make it with maybe an hour to spare. And the most relevant exchange:

IMOGEN: I've been chatting with their singer.

MOCHA: Since when?

IMOGEN: Since yesterday. She posted that they're auditioning for a new bass player. She said I was the first person to respond.

RICOCHET: What happened to their existing bass player? Spontaneous combustion?

IMOGEN: Didn't say. Just said her last show will be tonight in Houston and I should catch the show before she leaves.

MOCHA: Lucky!!

IMOGEN: I mean I do actually play the bass.

Oh, suuuuuuure there was a rational explanation. I mean, just because I demanded that Maxstacy promote this show to the entire internet and just because Imogen loves this band as much as I do and just because she lives within driving distance of the show and just because Susie's quitting the band and Imogen wants to audition because she actually plays the bass doesn't mean this ISN'T WEIRD—because twice now, I'd actually heard Airee's voice in my mind. Twice now, after long periods of poor to no sleep during which I soaked myself in brain-warping, behavior-altering music, I'd heard Airee's voice say creepy things in my mind and uh . . . hmm.

I got in the front seat of the van, put my laptop away, and put music on the stereo. I did not listen to Beautiful Remorse. I put on the Beatles and tried to relax.

A few minutes later, I stopped playing the Beatles, and listened to Beautiful Remorse.

• • •

After the show, the band's road crew pulled its van up to the loading dock and began ferrying out equipment. I could hear the headliner onstage in the distance. Normally the opening act in a small club waits to get its equipment out of the venue until after the entire show, but we were clearly in a hurry. Still, if the headliner was actually playing inside, the show couldn't have been a riotous fiasco like Austin.

The band itself appeared as a clump on the dock and hurriedly made their way to me, where I was idling the van, ready for a quick escape if it had been necessary. Maybe once or twice while I sat in the driver's seat of the idling van, scouring Google Maps for good fast routes out of town, it had occurred to me that something had gone very sideways with my overall life trajectory.

Sierra came up to the driver's side, knocked, and motioned for me to scoot over so she could drive.

"Where's Susie?" I asked, instantly suspicious.

"With the roadies," Sierra replied. "We're making room for Imogen to ride with Airee."

Airee and Imogen slid into the backseat behind us. The twins clambered in via the back doors and curled up with headphones, ignoring the rest of us. Sierra shifted into drive, and we were off.

The van was quiet. I spun slowly around in my seat and made eye contact with Imogen, for the first time ever unmediated by a computer screen.

"Hi," I said.

"Hi," she said.

I guess I was essentially just staring at Imogen at that point, which suddenly made me uncomfortable, so I turned to Airee and said, "I take it there were no riots tonight. Did you skip playing 'There Will Be Consequences'?"

Airee gave me a smug grin and said, "We played an acoustic version."

Within moments, Airee's head dipped, and she was sound asleep. Exhausted, more like—temporarily drained of whatever force animated her from moment to moment. Imogen didn't bat an eye. I turned to Sierra and asked, "Where are we headed?"

"Lawrence," she said quietly, indicating with her eyes I should shut up and let Airee sleep.

Maddening. I got on my phone and texted Imogen. Our first conversation in person was about to be held electronically.

"How was your interview?" I asked.

"They must like me because I'm joining the tour," she replied. "Debuting in Lawrence. Playing bass."

"Why did Susie Satori quit?" I typed indignantly, irritated that I myself didn't think to learn the bass twenty years ago.

"She didn't quit. She's dead."

"WHAT DO YOU MEAN, SHE'S DEAD?" I shouted out loud. Airee and the twins woke with a triplet of aggravated shrieks. Sierra swerved hard and pulled off the road.

"I thought you said she was with the roadies!"

"She is," Sierra responded calmly. "She's wrapped up in my drum rug, actually."

We were standing by the side of the van, she and I, obscured from the interstate, under the clear starry night somewhere in Texas. I was interrogating her; she was deflecting me.

"Did you people *kill* her back in Houston?"

"Oh listen to *you*," she said, suddenly venomous. "Now it's 'you people' as though you aren't complicit in everything we've done since you showed up."

"I'm not complicit in fucking *murder*!"

"We didn't murder anyone."

"Then why is she wrapped up in a fucking drum rug, Sierra?"

The road crew's van pulled up behind us on the shoulder. Sierra and I were suddenly immersed in its harsh interrogating headlight beams. Its driver jumped out and came over to us.

"Are we there yet?" said Susie Satori.

Before I could flip my shit and have a frustrated temper tantrum all over the place, the side door of the band van slid open, and Airee stepped into the cool night breeze in all her tempestuous glory. Meaning, a wind literally ripped across the highway at that moment, causing her hair and her scarf to swirl amazingly about her in a strange halo as she flipped me a thumb drive. I wasn't ready for it, so it bounced off my stomach and landed at my feet.

"That's a board recording of the new track from the show tonight," she said. "It's yours to release, just like we agreed."

"I'm not releasing anything until I understand what's going on here," I said.

"Bullshit," said Sierra quietly.

"You tried to convince me Susie was dead!"

"Just wanted to see how you'd handle yourself," Airee said. "Apparently you freak out at the first sign of trouble."

"Are you absolutely *kidding* me?" I snapped. "I watched people get crushed under a tower of loudspeakers and now I babysit your van while you're performing. Does that sound like freaking out?"

"Sounds like you're freaking out right this minute," she replied.

"I'm not freaking out! I'm just *frustrated* because you know more than you're telling me! Even Imogen is more in on it than me." I turned to Susie Satori. "By the way, Imogen says she's got your job. Did you know that?"

A confused expression lit up Susie's face. "Wait, what?"

"There's something *different* about your music, Airee," I continued, "something subliminal or, or—or I don't know what the other options are, but your music has a deeper neurological effect than it should and I want to know *how* you're doing it, and I want to know *why* you're doing it, or else I'm out. I'll go back home to Portland and Imogen can be your new *Herald*."

"*Herald*?" Imogen said. "What's that supposed to mean?"

"Why is she getting my job?" Susie protested.

"Just shut up," Airee said, looking at me but addressing all of us. "I'm only going to tell you this one more time.

I'm using my music to build a pool of psychic energy that I can tap into and use for taking over the planet. It won't be pretty if I succeed, and I'm already succeeding. But I've been building *so much* energy that I might instead be able to *escape* this shithole planet altogether. You should *hope and pray* I escape this shithole planet, really. Anyway, I realize this has been hard for all of you to accept. It's easy to lose sight of my personal mission in the middle of all the screaming crowds and the exhilarating violence. Maybe you need a more personal connection to what I'm doing. A more tangible demonstration of the *truth* of what I'm saying. Because let's be clear—you guys are the chosen few who get to witness what I'm doing, but nobody's safe on this tour, not even me, and you need to realize that right fucking now."

She jumped out and walked back to the road crew's van. I looked around at everyone, trying to gauge their reactions to the unbelievable line of bullshit Airee had just dumped on us. But Sierra could not have seemed more convinced, and I could tell that Imogen was more than half convinced. I studied my own reaction and realized that, holy shit, I might believe the line of bullshit myself and maybe that meant it wasn't bullshit and maybe that meant it *had* to be bullshit, didn't it? I mean, didn't it?

After a brief discussion with Airee, the road crew took off down the highway and disappeared, leaving us alone in the darkness. Airee sauntered back to us and said, "Sierra, take us to the first rest stop you can find."

"I'll drive," said Susie. She stormed around to the driver's side and got in. Airee and Sierra climbed into the backseat, crowded now with Imogen back there as well. I hesitated briefly but not sincerely, then picked up the thumb drive before climbing into the front passenger seat.

• • •

We parked in the darkest corner of the parking lot we could find. The road crew had parked here ahead of us. A few semitrucks idled in the distance, but for the most part, the rest stop we'd found was otherwise completely empty. Airee woke up the twins to make sure everyone was listening.

"We're going to listen to the new track," she said. "We were all wearing earplugs when we played it at the show, so this is the first time any of us will hear the live version without interference."

Everyone but possibly Imogen understood the significance of that statement.

The van had surprisingly good speakers for a car stereo system. The board recording may have been raw and unmastered, but it sounded fantastic. The new track was a mournful song that began slowly, wistfully, hazily. I felt like I had watched the tide recede, and was now looking at the wreckage left behind—knowing full well the tide would hit much harder when it soon returned. You could feel the music testing you, probing you, examining every molecule, every emotion, every secret thought, testing your reaction, testing your commitment, testing your heart. My heart was pounding, actually, the very stereotype of a pounding, frightened heart that anyone could hear from the other side of the closet door where you were hiding from the thing that was stalking you in the darkness.

I felt Imogen's mind brush against mine, just like when we'd listened to the second track together days ago, only much more intimate this time. She was scared too, but she was also thrilled and exhilarated. I got the impression she actually hadn't worn earplugs last night, and was hearing this song as Airee intended it, for a second time, and she was deeply enamored of the notion that she would be playing this music onstage tonight. Her enthusiasm was infectious. I wanted to hear her play this music myself. All I really wanted was to keep hearing this music, when you got right down to it. I couldn't remember why I'd had so many questions for Airee in the first place. She'd chosen me to announce this music to the world, and she'd chosen Imogen to play it alongside her.

We were among the blessed. Imogen felt relieved beyond measure that we were truly seeing things the same way.

When I finally opened my eyes and sat up, daylight was streaming in the windows. All around me, the others' heads lolled—they were all still in a trance, or maybe just asleep. All except Airee, who was gone.

"What's going on?" Sierra asked, rousing almost instantly. "Where's Airee?"

"I don't know. We've got to hit the road if we're going to make it to Lawrence in time," I told her. My determination quickly convinced her, and she roused the twins. I shook Susie's shoulder and tried to wake her, but she didn't stir. I shook her a little harder, a quick sharp bolt of realization stabbing me in the stomach as I did.

Susie was clearly dead. For real this time.

Airee threw open the back doors of the van. Sunlight streamed in behind her, giving her an insanely bright halo—not the angelic kind of halo, but rather the blinding, searing halo you get from staring directly into the sun. Her eyes seemed to be glowing too, and she was smiling and vibrating like she was fully charged again.

"What's that track called?" I asked her.

"It's called 'Some Were Not Meant to Last,'" Airee said. "Sierra, go get your drum rug."

Track 07

I finally met the band's road crew when we needed to figure out where to stash Susie Satori's body.

Sierra introduced me to Charlie, the band's guitar and drum tech, who seemed like she was barely out of high school; and Elsie, the band's live audio engineer, a chain smoker and clearly a bad influence on Charlie. It had been fairly easy to extract the drum rug from the back of the equipment van. It was much less obvious how we were going to reinsert the rug, now that a body was rolled up inside of it. This was one of those "loading van Tetris" problems you just never expect to have to solve. But Charlie and Elsie were both fairly relaxed about unloading gear and reloading it to accommodate the new cargo, and their reaction was telling.

"You were all expecting this," I said to Sierra as we walked back to the band van. "Airee knew that Susie 'wasn't meant to last,' is that it?"

"Susie kept talking about what she planned to do after the tour," Sierra replied.

"So?"

Either she pretended she didn't hear me, or she intended her silence to be her response. I wasn't satisfied.

"Who else isn't meant to last?" I pressed.

"Hard to say," she said. "*You* lasted longer than I thought you would."

. . .

I released "Some Were Not Meant to Last" as soon as we got back on the road again. I actually offered it to Maxstacy first. I owed him a favor for promoting the Houston show for me. He declined the honor.

"My whole mystique is that I'm the first to discover things," he said to me, "and this one's clearly yours. I didn't mind promoting the first show by 'the Augmented 4th,' but everyone knows you're the one who broke this band in the first place. If I start premiering their new tracks, people will think I stole them from you, and my credibility will tank."

So I posted the new track with my usual minimalistic critique and was about to drop off of Maxnet for the day when I saw some disturbing alerts in my news feeds. An epidemic had hit Houston overnight. Twelve people had died between 11 p.m. and early morning. No discernible cause, no overt symptoms—they simply fell asleep and didn't wake up. Eight other people had killed themselves—blown their brains out or slit their own throats.

Didn't take a background in epidemiology to predict that these people would all be traced back to a certain performance at the Nightingale Room. That'd happen even faster if the body of our former bass player turned up, plus the chances would then spike of connecting us sooner to the riot in Austin. So Susie had to stay with us for the time being. At least long enough for "Some Were Not Meant to Last" to start producing similar effects in people around the country, at which point things would become much more confusing from a disease vector perspective.

Yeah, I was definitely complicit at this point. I had been awakened by the undeniable presence of Airee Macpherson, and I had learned there would be consequences for veering off of her path. But I'd made a simple choice, and while some were clearly not meant to last, I wasn't going anywhere, not now. I would see this through to its finale, no matter the cost.

Or so I believed as we raced toward our next destination. Imogen spent the trip with her bass in her lap, crowded next to Airee in the backseat, practicing with her headphones on. Sierra stayed in the driver's seat, and for once in my life, I was relieved that she chose to leave the stereo off—ostensibly to make it easier for Imogen to practice, but the side effect was that my mind was a little more free to wander than it often had been during the stress of the past couple days.

With hours to go before we would arrive in Lawrence, I decided to find out everything I could about Airee Macpherson.

. . .

William had recognized Airee's name when I had first mentioned it on my channel, so presumably that meant she lived in Austin. Her Tumblr was called Undeniable Presence, but she used the URL aireemacpherson.tumblr.com, which is how I'd found her. On first glance, I hadn't really deduced much about her from skimming the surface of Undeniable Presence. That changed pretty quickly when I saw this post tucked away near the very beginning of the blog's existence:

> it's not like you wake up in the morning and decide you want to be the world's only living scholar in profane musicology
>   and by "living" i mean "surviving"

Her early posts on Undeniable Presence include a running thread where she's trying to convince her potentially imaginary readers that music is missing a proper notation system for a specific auditory illusion that she alone seems to understand. She coins the phrase "performative notation" to describe a theoretical system that more accurately captures the actual moment of inspiration experienced by a musician. She mentions in passing:

i guess some people go to their thesis adviser with ideas and actually get treated as though they are sane and full of promise

Suddenly she takes an unexpected detour off the rails completely, when she posts:

i went to a music conference in Madison, where this whole series of panels was dedicated to esoteric & mystical tuning systems, infernal chord progressions, centuries-old occult arrangements, all the weird stuff in music that they can't publish about in mainstream journals. and some schlub overheard my drunken ranting one night in the hotel bar about impossible music. and he said, "there's a recording you should hear." i said, "yeah, i doubt it." he said, "no, you should really hear it." i realized he was one of the speakers from earlier that day. he said, "this recording is a demo of you, singing from the future, a message back to you here in the present. i staged this whole conference just to attract you here so I could deliver this recording."

suddenly all the whiskey drained out of my veins and I stared the guy down, realizing he seriously believed what he was telling me. I said, "ok fine, let's hear this recording."

And then a few days later:

so let's just imagine for argument's sake that a future version of me sent me cryptic lyrical instructions from the future in a made-up language i've never heard but seem to
understand regardless. am i supposed to record this very
album so that it lasts long enough for future me to send it
back to me? time travel doesn't exist. if I'm so powerful in
the future that I can send arcane musical recordings back
into the past, why did I send them to some random schlub
to deliver to me? you see now why i didn't graduate

. . .

On Maxnet, something unexpected was happening. Ricochet had finally caved to pressure from Maxstacy, and was
actually listening to all of the Beautiful Remorse/Aug-
mented 4th tracks, in album order. He'd listened to enough
snippets of earlier tracks to be convincingly snarky, but now
he was taking them seriously. He was streaming his reactions live, to the relative delight of the channel.

As I watched, I received a DM from William, who was
finally able to connect.

"Glad you're okay," he said.

"Sorry I ditched you," I said. "It got scary and I bailed on you like a flat coward."

"Whatever—Maxstacy says you're on the road with them now, which is exactly the fuck where I would be if I were in your shoes, so stop worrying your pretty little head about me."

"What happened?"

"I blacked out from the pain, and didn't wake up until I came out of surgery, at which point I remained high on painkillers until—oh wait, I'm still high on painkillers."

Ricochet seemed transfixed as he heard track two, "The Awakening," for the very first time. I'd heard it dozens of times by now and I still felt transfixed, but it was exciting watching such an ardent denier become overwhelmed by it like we all had.

"Did anyone ask about us?" I finally worked up the guts to ask William.

"The split second the doc thought I was sufficiently conscious, I was grilled by a detective. But they weren't asking about you. They were asking about the big guy who started the riot."

"Huh?"

"The guy who elbowed you in the back, knocked you to the floor, remember that? And then I jumped in his face and tempers flared, and suddenly there was a riot?"

"But . . ."

"They saw the whole thing on security cam footage. Cop said I'm lucky I let the big guy throw me instead of punching him first, or I'd be facing some kind of felony charge right now."

We fell silent as Ricochet moved on to track three, "Undeniable Presence." A sense of quiet bliss overcame him. He muted the audio feed to our collective dismay, saying, "I don't mind if you people watch, but I need to keep the music for myself right now."

I should have said something to Ricochet about the music. But some days I really resented his snarky bullshit about all forms of music, and I thought if any music in the world could snap him out of that, this music would have to be it, right?

. . .

I took off my headphones, my ears needing a rest anyway. In the backseat, Imogen had moved on to practicing a bass line I didn't recognize. Quickly I deduced that Airee was teaching her tonight's new track. A chill jolted me. Even though I was only hearing one part in isolation, I was feeling slightly stunned. Imogen had her own headphones on; periodically she'd ask Airee a question or seek Airee's approval, and Airee's feedback was quick, concise, helpful.

"You guys won't have much time to rehearse with

Imogen when we get there," I said to Sierra.

"We don't rehearse," she replied. "Airee teaches us our parts individually. The first time we play the songs together is when we're onstage."

"Well, that'll be disappointing when it's time to release the box set," I said, cracking a silly joke to cover how inadequate I felt next to these apparently genius musicians. Or maybe all musicians in the world could and do learn music this way. I failed out of marching band in junior high because I literally could not figure out the cymbals, so it's my issue, I fully realize.

. . .

Ricochet got up from his computer, leaving his window momentarily empty.

"So they're not looking for us at all," I said to William.

"Didn't say that," he replied. "I have no idea. They just didn't ask me about you."

Think. Think back to what Sierra said when she found me in the hospital the next morning. Something about splitting town before the police realized what they'd seen on the video crew's footage? I couldn't remember exactly, and for a brief moment, I questioned everything I'd seen and felt. It all became suspect, for one brief shimmering moment. Maybe the riot in Austin was actually the result of a bad fight that broke out among amped-up bros. I was knocked to the floor; did I ever see anything else? Maybe Airee and Sierra had never actually been questioned by the police. How would I ever know without going back to Austin and turning myself in? Maybe the people who died in Houston were actually sick with a real disease. What if patient zero just happened to be in the audience last night? Maybe Susie Satori died of the same disease, or even natural causes. How could I know without delivering her body for an autopsy? Even the suicides—the CDC investigates clumps of suicides, so it's not unheard of.

Ricochet sat back down at his computer. He was weeping. Judging by the elapsed time, he was now most of the way through track six, "Some Were Not Meant to Last." He put a large kitchen knife to his throat and jammed it straight through his jugular.

· · ·

The band all disappeared into tonight's venue, the Bottleneck, leaving me alone in the van again. Before she followed the others, I managed to pull Imogen aside for an actual face-to-face conversation. It was very awkward, and amounted to very little. Airee hadn't been surprised when I told her that hundreds of people around the country were dying mysteriously or killing themselves and I thought it was because they were listening to track six. Imogen didn't care that she would be playing the whole album tonight, including the deadly track six and the currently unpredictable track seven. I didn't care that I'd be waiting in the getaway van again, ready as ever to release track seven onto the internet as soon as we were a safe distance from Lawrence.

I did care that Imogen might get hurt, though. I told her as much. She didn't care.

"Ricochet killed himself," I told her. "Didn't make it through track six."

I'm not sure what reaction I expected. Neither one of us knew Ricochet except as a slightly humorous, frequently annoying internet presence. But when you boiled it right down, Imogen and I didn't know each other much better, no matter what we pretended while we were long-distance internet buddies.

"What if you don't make it through track seven?" I asked.

"You don't play, so you don't understand," she replied. "I don't *care* if I make it through. Playing that music with her, even one time, is worth everything to me."

"C'mon, 'everything'?" I countered. "That's a lot of things."

"You said it yourself—she shouldn't be able to do the things she's doing with this music. She's unlocked something huge, and I get to play a role in expressing it. You could live your whole life as a mediocre artist who never gets a chance to affect the world the way she is."

"She's arguably not having the best effect," I said.

"Then why don't you quit the tour? Or try to stop her?"

Quit the tour? That would be like gouging out my eardrums. No way. And trying to stop her—it sounded ridiculous just thinking about it. The damage she was doing to the world was incidental to making sure I heard the rest of the album.

I said, "What's the new track called?"

"I'm not supposed to tell you," she said. But after a quick pause, she said, "It's called 'The Price of Adoration.'"

. . .

Around 10:15 p.m., a blazing portal of energy opened directly above the venue. It seemed wide enough to swallow up the entire city block. I heard a profoundly unsettling shriek from all around me and nearly puked from sudden fear.

Moments later, I saw Airee, Sierra, and the twins sprinting toward me, screaming the whole way.

I did not see Imogen.

Track 08

Before the band reached the van, an enormous clawed appendage unfurled from the portal, descending toward the venue and smashing through the roof. It was a long barbed arm of some kind, flexible in certain ways like a tentacle, but jointed in spots where bones might lurk beneath the rotting spongy skin. My lizard brain was locked in a terror loop, unable to move, thoroughly frozen in the face of something so massive, so impossible, so ungodly.

Sierra slammed into the side of the van and threw the driver's door open, but I couldn't move. She shoved me and shoved me again, but I wouldn't move.

The appendage smashed through the side of the venue, ripping one entire wall down, and I watched human bodies fly through the air under the pallid streetlights, screaming as they flew. I heard myself bawling and babbling but I couldn't understand what I was saying and I didn't feel connected to my body—even more so than usual.

And then, with no ceremony and no warning, the portal suddenly disappeared—thankfully—severing the appendage from its unlucky owner. The appendage flopped down hard from its great height and smashed half a city block's worth of buildings. It was sheer fate that caused it to flop facing the other direction from where the van was parked; we would've easily been crushed to death before I could've gotten the van moving in my state.

A brief silence followed, and then wails and shrieks rose up from the debris field where the venue once stood. And inexplicably, in the midst of the dawning horror of the night's events, Airee began laughing. She strolled around and climbed in the passenger seat of the van. Sierra and the twins quietly climbed in back.

"That was *so close!*" she shouted, cackling. "You guys, that was *so close!*"

"Close to what?" I asked.

"Close to opening a portal to my home dimension!" she said, as though she was shouting the most obvious fact in the history of shouting facts. "I missed the target and wound up opening a portal to who-knows-what-the-fuck dimension, which yes, *that* was a problem, because apparently giant tentacled beasts live there. And now they know about your planet, although who knows if they can find their way here. But the point is, we were *so close!* I swear we'll get it right tomorrow night!"

"Drive the van," Sierra ordered.

Many things go through your mind when you realize

the entire world is very obviously doomed. This prevented me from driving the van.

"What happened to Imogen?" I asked.

"*That's* what you care about?" Airee replied, incredulous. "After what you just saw?"

"She's not coming," Sierra said quietly. "You should drive the van."

I heard the sirens of emergency vehicles in the distance, and for some reason, the very realistic threat of the Lawrence police department was able to motivate me to get moving. Brain could comprehend "going to jail" in ways it couldn't comprehend "end of the world by giant sky claw."

I fired up the van and kicked it into gear. As I pulled onto the road and began to accelerate, I realized too late that a large man was standing in the road directly in front of me. I was going to hit him before I'd ever get the chance to apply the brakes. It didn't matter. He threw an incredible punch that smashed the front of the van into a crumpled mess and stopped our forward momentum completely. We weren't going fast, obviously, but I still hit the steering wheel hard with my head, and Airee flew forward against the dashboard. When I stopped seeing stars, I realized that the man standing in the glow of the one remaining headlight was the man from the show in Austin, the big guy who had elbowed me to the ground.

He looked a lot angrier than the last time I'd seen him.

Airee looked up to get her bearings, pure fury on her face, as the man strode around to her side of the van and began to pull the passenger door off completely. She timed it perfectly to kick him hard in the face once the door was gone, and he staggered backward onto the shoulder of the road. The twins popped out of the side door of the van and savagely attacked him, knocking him onto his back before he could get his balance after Airee's kick. As they proceeded to pound him into submission, Airee climbed on top of the van, where she could survey the entire scene: the wreckage of the venue, the enormous tentacle that lay splattered down the center of the neighborhood, the struggling man who was currently subdued by the twins but was rapidly regaining his wits. I saw Sierra put her earplugs in, and I rapidly followed suit.

The man tried to shout something at Airee. It came out as a muffled, hoarse bleating sound, like cattle being mutilated, but slowed to half speed.

"Is that all you got, open mic night?" Airee said with a laugh. "Let me show you what a real singer can do."

She sang a melody I thought I recognized, which quickly and suddenly transformed into a horrifying sonic wave of pure antipathy. The man's head briefly swelled, then exploded, showering the twins with gore.

I passed out.

. . .

When I awoke, the world was very different.

I was alone in the back of the road crew van. Music was playing. It wasn't coming out of the car stereo though. It was outside, playing at a significant volume. I'd never heard it, but I recognized its signature immediately. This was Beautiful Remorse. Or the Augmented 4th—whatever you wanted to call them. I suspected I was hearing the new track, somehow recorded at the show before it was rudely interrupted by a massive death strike from another dimension. I recognized Imogen's bass line, the one and only time she'd perform it for an audience. It was an achingly beautiful song, and it filled me with energy, like I was a video game character who'd reached a health station and was topping off.

I climbed out of the van. Dawn was coming on fast. Airee Macpherson owned Lawrence, Kansas.

. . .

I staggered through the streets. Somehow, the music was sufficiently amplified so that you could hear it all throughout the city. I could hear it vibrating inside my own skull, contributing to the effect. It was exactly like Sierra had said at the hospital in Austin: my brain was a battery in the energetic network that Airee controlled and used for sustenance. They were playing the entire album in order up through track seven, waking these people up to Airee's music and capturing them in its web.

The streets were filled with people staggering about in varying degrees of shock. Every time track six came up, a few people here and there would suddenly die and collapse, or violently kill themselves with whatever implement was handy, and you got very immune to seeing it over time.

. . .

I would have expected some kind of coordinated police response, maybe? Something big to put a stop to all this chaos—the National Guard maybe? Something with enough firepower to hold off the next giant death tentacle from the sky? Then I wondered what was happening across the country if track seven had gotten out. My phone was dead so I couldn't check. But let's imagine track seven was out. The track itself couldn't be the trigger that opened up the portal, or we'd have a portal every forty-five minutes right here in Lawrence.

Track seven plus a *sacrifice*, however . . .

What if this was happening all over the country?

. . .

I saw my first runner a few hours later. Someone who was completely unaffected by the music, who wasn't existentially destroyed by track six, someone who was terrified and caught in the middle of a strange and sudden hell on earth. She was running from two quick pursuers, who rapidly caught her and slammed her to the ground. I recognized the pursuers: it was the twins.

Except they looked very different. Enhanced somehow—bigger, more muscular, meaner, more ferocious. They smiled at me and I realized they were both demons of some kind. I don't think they started off as demons, but they were definitely past the point of no return at this point.

"There you are," they said in creepy unison, because of course they did. Their prey scampered off while their attention was on me. "Airee's been looking all over for you."

. . .

They led me back to the epicenter of the destruction, where a small crew of individuals was erecting a makeshift stage—setting up generators, loudspeakers, instruments, the works. Airee was planning another show tonight. They still had three tracks to release before the album was complete.

If they were looking for me, maybe that meant she hadn't released track seven yet. Maybe she still expected her *Herald* to do that.

Sierra was waiting for me at a park bench near the new stage.

"Snagged this from the band van," she said, handing me my backpack. "Thought you might want that."

I studied her very, very closely, looking for any signs that Sierra had transformed like the twins. Then, almost as an afterthought, I took a close look again at the twins. They looked just like they always had. Normal, cute, bored. My head was pounding with pain, from when I hit the steering wheel. Or maybe from the aggressively loud music that was constantly playing throughout the city. Some percentage of what I was feeling was imaginary bullshit and the rest of it was abject terror. I sat down on the bench and opened my backpack, to find my laptop secure inside.

"Thank you for finding him," Sierra said. The twins nodded but loitered nearby.

We sat together silently for a while, observing our surroundings. I felt like I was seeing the aftermath of a hurricane even though all but a few of the buildings in town were still standing.

"Where's Airee?" I said.

"Recruiting a new bass player," she told me.

"Jesus fucking Christ," I said, starting to rise. Behind me, the twins forcibly shoved me back onto the bench. Got it—so it's like that.

"She wants you to post track eight," she said, handing me yet another deadly thumb drive.

"What about track seven?"

"We posted it last night while you were passed out."

"When did you record track eight?"

"We haven't. This is Airee's demo. She was hoping to record it last night as well, but the show got a little inter-rupted."

"Obviously you guys can post it without my help," I said.

"She likes it better when you do it. She says having a *Herald* is classy."

"Oh for fuck's sake—"

"This is the wrong time to get mouthy. Just shut up and listen. You need to post the new track immediately. Spread the word about what happened here. Tell the truth, who gives a fuck what you say. Then you're going to figure out how to operate a sound board, because Elsie got herself accidentally killed last night."

"As opposed to the people who got killed on purpose last night?"

"Yes. *Exactly.* As opposed to the people who might *still* get killed on purpose, in fact."

I imagined I could hear the twins snickering behind us,

but I was clearly delusional about most things by this point.

I pulled out my laptop and fired it up. My hotspot still worked. Out of instinct, I dared to check my email before doing anything else. There was a message from Sierra Nelson waiting for me with the subject line: "What happens next."

They killed Imogen during the show last night. Airee and the twins. Airee's music is a psychic virus unleashed on the world, but blood sacrifice onstage is what's making Airee herself stronger, and she's not done yet. I'm pretty sure they're going to kill me during the show tonight. If the world is still standing after that, I'm pretty sure they're going to kill you during the show tomorrow night. No one is coming to rescue us. No one knows how she summoned that thing from the sky but she has them convinced she can do it again whenever and wherever she wants. We need to get out of Lawrence fast. I guess that's probably obvious. I'm open to suggestions. First you should post the new track. We'll never survive the rest of the day if she doesn't see that track go live on Much Preferred Customers soon.

"What's track eight called?" I asked her.
"It's called 'Destroy All Unbelievers,'" she said.

Track 09

Posting a new track was a five-minute process, top to bottom, from booting the machine to pushing the publish button. I decided to make some pleasant small talk to pass the time.

"Who the fuck was that guy whose head exploded?" I asked.

"Airee won't tell us," Sierra said. "She admits someone's been stalking her but she won't say who and she won't say why."

"Yeah but . . . she made that guy's head explode!"

"I know. But to be fair, he punched out our van!"

"His head exploded! That is not fair!"

"I am not the boss of Airee Macpherson!"

We were shouting a lot. We both still had our earplugs in. I suspected we would never take them out again as long as we lived. Which wasn't super likely to be that much longer anyway.

As soon as my laptop connected, I fired up Maxnet. The main channel was a ghost town. I DM'd William but got no response. For kicks, I DM'd Maxstacy as well, and also got no response. My feeds were showing me the national news reporting about some kind of natural disaster in Lawrence—and also in Austin, Chicago, Mexico City, Sydney, Vancouver, and Bristol. People were calling it a "natural disaster" despite dozens of iPhone videos of giant sky tentacles smashing buses and churches and any goddamn thing they felt like smashing.

Was Airee the epicenter of this apocalypse, or just one of the spokes?

Did Airee actually have any control, or was she just making sacrifices to the unknowable out of blind stupid devotion? Or worse, because she just wanted to see what the fuck might happen?

Her blog post had said that some schlub at a music conference had delivered a demo recording to her in a bar. Who the fuck was that schlub, how much did he fucking know, and where the fuck was he now?

I considered what kinds of trouble I could get into by uploading an old Neil Diamond track and claiming it was the new Beautiful Remorse track. The twins were watching closely as I composed the post. I finished uploading the new track. Normally I would add some cryptic but pithy commentary, something intriguing to entice listeners, but I no longer needed any such pretense whatsoever. Instead I simply wrote: "Here is the new Beautiful Remorse track. It's called 'Destroy All Unbelievers.' I'm not in any way encouraging anyone to do any actual destroying. You probably know and love a few unbelievers yourself and I suspect they would prefer it if you did not destroy them." I was terrified of what mayhem I had just unleashed. I swore that this would be my last act as Airee's *Herald,* even if she killed me for it. I realized I wouldn't have the guts to disobey her if she were standing here in front of me though. I was despondent.

The twins saw the post go live from over my shoulder. Satisfied, they wandered off in search of a new diversion. They shouted back to Sierra, "Don't miss sound check!"

Suddenly Maxstacy responded to my DM.

"Holy shit you're alive!" he said.

"So are you!" I said.

"Yeah but I'm not the one on tour with a homicidal alien-summoning cult leader!"

"It sounds so quaint when you put it like that."

"I can't believe you released a new track."

"If you were here, you'd believe anything."

"That's my point—you must know by now what that music is doing to people!"

"Yes. Obviously. Wait, are you immune?"

"I haven't listened to any of it. I have no idea if I'm immune and I don't plan to find out. Are you still in Lawrence?"

"For now."

"Are you in danger?"

"Of course I'm in danger."

"Imminent danger?"

"Yes, if I stay here, I am going to die here."

Maxstacy fell silent, one of those "Maxstacy is typing . . ." moments where he probably just went to the bathroom. I looked over at Sierra, who was not at all attempting to hide that she was reading the entire conversation on my screen. Impatiently I flipped over to news feeds for a moment, and found myself distraught to learn that roving bands of murderers were out in the streets of major cities around the world with boom boxes blasting Beautiful Remorse. Converting the masses, exterminating the immune. Sierra finally made eye contact with me. When this tour started, Sierra was all in, and now she was racked with guilt. Like me. For all the good it could do.

"I think you should get out of Lawrence," Maxstacy finally said, "and come here. Do you have wheels?"

Sierra said, "Charlie's got the key to the crew van."

My mind reeled. I'd seen too many TV shows, or not enough. Airee could summon space tentacles by killing bass players. Could she command the state patrol to chase down her crew van? Fuck it, who cared.

"Yeah, we have wheels," I told him. "Where are you?"

"I'm in Madison."

Madison, Wisconsin, where Sierra and I went to

school together without knowing each other, where Sierra's band Surrealist Sound System first captured my imagination and set me on the righteous path toward music blogging, where Airee Macpherson attended the music conference that changed her life. I wanted desperately to believe this was a coincidence.

"What a coincidence," I said.

. . .

We had to trick Charlie into giving us the key to the crew van. And by trick I mean punch. We left her tied up in somebody's garage and took off. No one stopped us. Not sure anyone even noticed us. It's not like this was martial law. It's not like cameras were everywhere. It's not like some secret police force was out hunting for us. It was simply that at any given moment giant alien tentacle beasts might descend from the sky and slaughter us.

Even that assumption was starting to wear off. The more distance I got from Airee, the more I realized that the portal in the sky and the subsequent giant alien tentacle beast were summoned as part of a ritual—one that likely involved spilling blood, and one that definitely involved performing Airee's music. By stealing Sierra—tonight's drummer and probable sacrifice—I was dealing Airee quite a setback to any immediate plans she might have to summon a giant alien tentacle beast. Shit, even if her new bass player was ready to go on tonight, it seemed increasingly unlikely that a new drummer could go on too.

Normally my favorite part of posting a track was watching all the responses pile up: the plays and likes and reblogs. Today the cycle was massively accelerated. I'd never seen a post go so disturbingly viral. Probably because people were discovering that the track "Destroy All Unbelievers" sounded exactly like the Monkees track "I'm a Believer." Don't ask me why I have Monkees tracks on my laptop. The point is the twins were too stupid to spot me switching out the track in my post.

Who knew when Airee would realize all of this, but we'd be hours away before she even had a clue which direction we'd gone.

We drove through the night to get to Madison, stopping once to get gas at a weird truck stop where we couldn't tell if the people there were just normally this weird or if tonight was an actual change of pace. We took turns interrogating each other as we drove in silence, neither of us in the mood for any kind of traditional road trip music.

"If you've never met this guy, why do you trust him?" she asked me.

That was a good question. How close could you be

with someone you only knew via some obscure darknet?

"I trust him as much as I trust anyone on Maxnet," I replied. "The people I really trust are all in Portland or back home in Colorado, and nobody is answering my texts or my emails." I hated saying that out loud. "But without Maxstacy, I never would have . . ."

Met Imogen, is what I didn't say. But she caught on anyway.

"Were you and Imogen close?"

I said, "It hurts like we were close."

"I guess that counts for something."

I changed the subject. "How did you wind up in a band with a demon-summoning blood priestess?"

"She was in Madison the year after I graduated, doing some research for her doctorate. She caught one of Surrealist Sound System's final shows and started hitting on me afterward. I guess I'm a sucker for attention."

"Like most rock stars," I said. "When did you realize Airee was out to destroy the world?" In my mind, that was the money question. When did Sierra give in to the dark side? And was it just pure self-interest that had snapped her out of it?

"When she played me her demos for the first time, I wanted more than anything to play that music as loud and as hard as I could, for as long as I could . . . I think I knew subconsciously right then and there that she wasn't planning anything wholesome."

"She believes she sent those demos to herself from the future."

"She believes a lot of very weird shit, and a lot of it is turning out to be true."

"Who did she get the demos from, do you know? On her blog, she said it was just some schlub." I paused, then said, "If Maxstacy turns out to be a schlub when we meet him, let's be prepared to get back in this fucking van immediately."

· · ·

Maxstacy turned out to be a schlub. We decided not to get back in the van immediately.

I mean the classic definition of a schlub is a little unflattering, and Airee was probably being a dick when she called him that. He was fine. He was an old dude, a professor of musicology. He lived alone in a small cottage on the edge of Madison city limits, and he seemed quite happy to have company.

Oh sure, he was not expecting Sierra. I'm pretty sure I intentionally neglected to mention she was coming with me, although there's a chance I honestly forgot because I was busy freaking out about the whole end of the world thing. But he was gracious, and he welcomed us both in.

I never would have guessed that Maxstacy was this old professor dude, but in retrospect, his blog was always so incredibly articulate and erudite. All of us looked up to Maxstacy not simply because he was first on the scene, but because he continued to earn his place of honor with year after year of highly intelligent pop music critique. I mean we all have differences in taste, we're all music snobs to each other about something along the way, but Maxstacy was considered the best because he truly, unabashedly loved pop music—he was never simply posing.

"Yes, she got those demo recordings from me," he admitted without reservation as we sat around his kitchen table and shared a bottle of wine. "Begging the question, I'm sure, of where exactly did I get them originally. You may not realize—my dissertation was on the intersection of musicology and occultism. The occult is a fringe area within the humanities to be sure, but it produces historical artifacts that can and should be studied—including charts of music. Black hymns used in profane rituals, diabolic tuning systems, theosophical symphonies, that sort of rubbish. Worth studying because, as with any area of music, every now and then some genius comes along and for a brief shining moment makes that whole sliver of the musical firmament light up with unexpected beauty.

"Occultists used to collect and trade these charts,

much as we collect vinyl recordings from thrift shops today. It was a tough racket—you'd see handwritten charts claiming to be old Egyptian necromantic hymns and you'd have to speculate—is this some shitty bootleg or is this the real deal? Huge fortunes were quietly spent on this stuff. Anyway, eventually a significant collection wound up in the hands of John Dee, who was Queen Elizabeth's court alchemist and astrologer at the time. Dee himself had no particular affinity for music, beyond fancying himself a mathematician. And he didn't trust his sight reading. His idea for establishing the provenance of the charts was to hire musicians and actually hear the music out loud. Ten specific charts were chosen for this command performance, to be played on ten successive nights by various combinations of court musicians and guest virtuosos from around the British Empire.

"I have reason to believe that John Dee did not survive the entirety of these performances. Oh, certainly someone or something using Dee's identity survived until the early 1600s. But what occurred even as early as Dee first laying eyes on those charts was a nonconsensual communion with an extradimensional entity that used infernal music as a gateway channel into our reality. These entities need hosts to survive here. They prime human minds for their arrival using these occult charts as extradimensional tuning forks, so to speak, until the hosts are sufficiently pliant to accept them without resistance.

"I have reason to believe this because I myself am hosting one of these entities, and before the barbiturates in your wine wear off, you will each be hosting one as well."

Track 10

When I awoke, I was extremely groggy. At first I thought it was due to the amount of wine I'd had to drink. Then I belatedly remembered my wine had been spiked with barbiturates. In fact, I'd watched Sierra nod off before Maxstacy had even finished his little monologue and thought to myself, *How odd, I never would have expected a rock-and-roll drummer to be such a lightweight,* before realizing I too was feeling the effects of the wine much faster than I anticipated. And now here I was, waking up feeling groggy and realizing I'd been drugged.

Physically, I was tied to a chair, gagged, and listening to what sounded like a gramophone recording of an ensemble of medieval musicians. Instead of a single lead singer, several male and female musicians traded lead, duet, and chorus duties. I recognized the melody but couldn't immediately place it. Mentally, a building fury threatened to crowd my consciousness out completely, and I struggled to maintain a presence inside my own mind.

Across the room, Sierra was also tied to a chair, growling and occasionally shrieking through her gag. She sounded feral, or insane, or both.

"The music you're hearing is the infamous Viereck recording of the Ten Charts," Maxstacy said genially, making conversation as though this was all very normal to him. "We're up to the Fifth Chart," he continued. "Normally the process takes a bit less time, but you are well acquainted with the major themes in these charts, so I'm not surprised to see that you've built some resistance."

Resistance?

Then it clicked. The Fifth Chart was a variation on the melody of Airee's track five—"You've Been Given a Simple Choice." Maxstacy thought he was doing something specific to me by playing these Viereck recordings. Clearly it was having an effect on Sierra—or was it? I could have sworn that when Maxstacy wasn't looking, she stopped seizing long enough to smile and wink at me, before going back to her act.

"The woman you know as Airee Macpherson is actually a psychopathic criminal from the future," Maxstacy said, and I swear, when you hear someone say a thing like that with no trace of irony and you believe it almost immediately, you really do wonder about the choices you've made in life. But then, of course, he had to take it to an even more fucked-up place. "She's been expelled from her home dimension, banished hundreds of millions of years into the past, into a proto-primitive mind on a proto-primitive world where no recognizable culture could be said to exist from her perspective. A prison, in other words, where she could do no further harm to her home society, where she would live out the rest of a frail human lifetime in anguish at what she had lost and would never see again. Her consciousness will be extinguished and dispersed when the host body dies. This is a life sentence and a death sentence all rolled into one."

What did that make Maxstacy? A prison guard? Why would they need one? To admit new inmates, or . . . or to keep the inmates from destroying the prison.

Like Airee Macpherson was busy doing. Shit.

Maxstacy flipped the vinyl recording over to side B, and soon enough a sparse, haunting arrangement of the Sixth Chart—"Some Were Not Meant to Last"—began. This chart was a culling. Maxstacy could use it to eliminate those who arrived here and refused to cooperate with his orders. What was he expecting from me?

Sierra was still choking and gagging across the room—damned convincing. I'd missed the boat on pretending to have seizures—which, let's be clear, looked pretty exhausting anyway—but I did introduce a little twitch into my tied-up hands and feet, while I considered how to get out of this mess.

Maxstacy finally removed my gag.

"Now perhaps you understand my business here,"

he said. "I locate the hosts and prime them with the Ten Charts. The Viereck recordings are the most famous, but many variations exist—some from the past, some from the future. Airee Macpherson managed to steal a set of recordings from me and she's twisting them to her own purpose. I would say she must be punished for her crime, but being here is already punishment. No, she must be *destroyed,* like any who disregard my authority."

I was inclined to believe him.

"The last individual I sent to stop Airee Macpherson broke off contact suddenly," Maxstacy continued. "I suspect you know what happened to my weapon, yes? Go on, you can answer—I see you haven't yet lost your human identity."

"She made your weapon's head explode with her voice," I said. "After he punched out our van."

Maxstacy actually seemed to be surprised by that idea. Then he regained his composure and said, "You are part of her inner circle. You could get *close* to her."

"Uh, not after spending the last ten hours getting *away* from her," I said. "She's not going to trust me now."

We both looked over at Sierra, who had slumped into apparent unconsciousness.

"And I don't think Sierra is secret-agent material," I concluded.

The Seventh Chart began, which I knew as the track "The Price of Adoration"—the one track that Imogen had managed to play with the band. Rehearsing it in the van all day, she'd gone over to Airee completely somehow, and I felt that same pull toward Maxstacy as I listened to this recording.

I said, "Why are the titles of her songs in English, but her lyrics are gibberish?"

"Airee's using a bit of creative license with her titles," Maxstacy replied. "Probably for SEO reasons. But the lyrics are hardly gibberish. It's what John Dee incorrectly identified as an angelic language called Enochian. It's actually the military patois of our race, a command-and-control language that can override sentient free will."

"Seems like she's still got plenty of free will. But the versions that she's playing and releasing don't sound anything like this recording of yours."

"Yes, she's definitely found a way off script in several ways. And her results have been quite unexpected. Hence my deep desire to find a way to bring her back into the fold."

The Eighth Chart, which I had never heard before, began, and I fell silent, absorbing the musical information with full concentration. This was the song Airee called "Destroy All Unbelievers," which I had pretended to post to my blog but hadn't actually heard. As

I listened, Maxstacy's desire to bring Airee back into the fold was magnified by my own personal desire to destroy her. She was perverting an entire system of justice, and I realized at that moment how much I absolutely hated her for what she was doing to this innocent world (which was a far cry from the typical nihilistic loathing I felt about the planet).

I said, "How can I help you? She's gotten so strong. Even if I managed to get close to her, she'd overpower me in a heartbeat. Plus she's got the twins. And she can summon death tentacles from the sky!"

He said, "Just listen. You must listen."

And the Ninth Chart began. I'd never heard something so unexpectedly hopeful. In the midst of such a menacing arsenal of musical compositions—music capable of bending the minds of extradimensional aliens and destroying the minds of unfortunate humans at the same time, music capable of twisting Airee Macpherson from a mixed-up musicology student into a despotic heavy-metal warlord—somehow the Ninth Chart showered me with the tiniest hints of light. If I had to give it a cheesy English title, I'd call it "You've Been Given a Second Chance."

"I don't understand," he said at last, clearly frustrated with me. "You should have become a host by this point in the music, but clearly you're only susceptible to *her* version of this music now."

"Wait—maybe I don't *want* to be a host!"

"They are sending me another weapon!" he exclaimed. "A stronger one—a true warrior! One of you must be ready to accept it! But the woman you brought with you is useless, and you yourself are not much better. What will I do?"

"Why don't *you* be the fucking host?" I said. "If they're sending a fucking weapon, why don't *you* save the world?" I was really getting warmed up. "What kind of *coward* are you?"

"I can't risk myself in such a fight!" he exclaimed. "Without me, who would awaken the prisoners to their new lives?"

"You mean, who would obliterate a bunch of innocent people by dumping extradimensional psychopaths from the future into their minds?" That's when it hit me—if they were sending messages and prisoners back from the goddamn future, this whole thing was already a foregone conclusion, so what the fuck were we even doing here?

The matter was resolved for us by a single massively amplified guitar chord coming from outside the cottage. Maxstacy's eyes widened as he crossed to the window and peered out through the curtain.

"Of course," he murmured. "She followed you straight to me."

"YOU'VE GOT MY DRUMMER," Airee's unmistakable voice growled over whatever ridiculous sound system she'd brought with her "AND YOU'VE GOT MY HERALD. I WANT THEM BACK!"

Sierra sat up in her chair, pulled her gag off, and smiled. Her hands were untied; that's what she had been working on during her entire bullshit seizure routine.

Maxstacy threw open the curtains so that we could both see clearly what was happening outside. A flatbed semitrailer was parked on the lawn, and Beautiful Remorse was set up on top of it between two towers of loudspeakers. They started vamping on an introduction as they saw Maxstacy standing in his living room. It was the twins on keys and guitar, a wobbly but competent new bass player, a staggering array of drum machines and samplers, and a defiant Airee Macpherson, somehow bathed in a spotlight.

Oh wait—that wasn't a spotlight, that was a portal of energy starting to open directly above her head.

"I'M HERE TO PLAY TRACK NINE FOR YOU," she said. "USING EVERY PROFANE TECHNIQUE I LEARNED FROM STUDYING YOUR FUCKED-UP CHARTS OF MISERY AND DOOM, TRACK NINE IS MY MASTERPIECE, THE ABSOLUTE HIGHLIGHT OF MY ALBUM. WOULD YOU LIKE TO KNOW WHAT IT'S CALLED?"

Maxstacy shook his head. No ma'am, he did not want to know.

"IT'S CALLED 'YOU ARE ABOUT TO DIE, MOTHERFUCKER!'"

Maxstacy didn't respond. But I knew better what was potentially about to happen and had zero interest in my head exploding. Any vocal assault that could take down Maxstacy was going to catch Sierra and me in its wake.

"Sierra, we have to get out of here!" I shouted.

"Chill the fuck out!" she shouted back.

And then, with an immensely powerful screech, Airee Macpherson began singing her masterpiece, "You Are About to Die, Motherfucker."

An astounding wall of sound hit the house, and for a second I thought I was going to vomit. But as the song progressed, Maxstacy took the brunt of the punishment. His skin started to blacken and peel, and he started to glow from the inside, as though he were turning into a radioactive melon. He didn't just stand there and take it though. He opened his mouth, took an enormous breath, and then retaliated with his own epic samurai warrior death song. I couldn't hear it well enough to pick out a melody in what he was doing, so if he was singing the Tenth Chart, it was lost on me. But it seemed to have an effect. I heard feedback from the stage and the sound of what might have been a speaker exploding. A desperate musicological duel was underway, one that would clearly end with complete obliteration for at least one of the participants. With such a sonic maelstrom surrounding us, it was a miracle that Sierra and I survived.

Actually, it was earplugs, which we were still wearing. Which we'd been wearing the entire time Maxstacy was trying to prime us with the Viereck recordings.

And let me just throw in a quick shout-out for the Moldex Pura-Fit earplugs, providing the highest noise reduction rating (33 db) you can get in a disposable earplug. Some "high-fidelity" earplugs with lower NRR (let's say 12 to 20 db) reduce noise evenly across the spectrum in a way that allows music and vocals to shine through while still providing healthy noise reduction otherwise; they're often considered great concert earplugs for that reason. But make the jump to the 33 db earplugs, trust me. It's the most noise reduction you can get for any reasonable amount of money short of having your ears filled with molten lead, and it's worth it for extending the life of your hearing. And in our case, extending the life of our lives. I mean, certainly we still heard and felt Airee's music when it was aimed our direction. Earplugs can only ever block air-conducted noise, but bone-conducted noise will always get through; there's no body armor version of an earplug. So yeah, we definitely suffered.

But Maxstacy eventually lost that duel. His entire body melted into gore and then ash by the time the song was over. He fought well enough that she couldn't just make his head explode like a water balloon, but in the end, he might have suffered less if he hadn't fought the way he had.

Sierra untied me, and we went outside onto the lawn, where the portal in the sky above Airee was now wide open. I nearly fainted from sheer terror at the giant war machine gingerly stepping through the portal and setting down on the lawn next to Airee's semitrailer. It was maybe three stories tall, a mechanized exoskeleton around some kind of mutated flying dinosaur, with five spindly arachnid legs holding up its trunk. No head, no eyes, no mouth—just a giant cyborg spider beast, covered in dripping acidic ooze, hanging out on the lawn. Rows of hooks and planks hung down from the exoskeleton; this thing was clearly a troop transport.

Airee smiled when she saw us. "You got here just in time," she said. "I've organized a prison break." The twins were already climbing onto the beast. "As you might guess, this portal goes to the *right* dimension. You're both invited to join me on my triumphant return home."

Sierra and I exchanged a quick look. I realized I knew absolutely nothing about Sierra's life after she graduated. Nothing about whether she had friends or family or any kind of connection to this world. I certainly didn't qualify. She said nothing and took off toward Airee.

The new bass player had passed out in a heap. Sierra stepped over her; she would someday wake up and be relieved or mortified to learn they'd left her behind on this planet.

"Are you joining us, *Herald*?" Airee asked. "Or is this tiny planet suitable for your limited ambition?"

I was surprised to learn that I was tempted. Very, very tempted. But something in Airee's eyes conveyed her intent very clearly: the world she was heading back to was not going to enjoy her reappearance, not one bit.

I tried and failed to think of something meaningfully human to say or do. She laughed—not mocking, almost affectionate.

"Do you know why I'm here?" she asked with a grin. "My crime was stealing the knowledge of my enemies and wiping their existence from the very fabric of reality. I know many things."

"Not enough to avoid being caught?"

"Enough to avoid being caught *twice*." She flipped a thumb drive through the air at me. I wasn't ready; it bounced off my chest and landed at my feet. "It's track ten. Your reward for serving as my *Herald*. If you ever decide you want to finish raining down hell on this little world, post track ten on your internet, and I will hear it.

I will return, and we will finish what we started here. We will take this world for ourselves, once and for all."

But she was from the future—she already knew what I was going to do with track ten, even if I myself didn't yet know.

She leapt up onto the spider beast, which leapt up through the portal, which disappeared, leaving only the cool night air in its wake. And leaving a semitrailer parked on the lawn of a disintegrated music professor, and leaving a passed-out bass player from Lawrence, and leaving the rest of the country still freaking out about the weird music she'd left behind on the internet, and leaving the military freaked out about portals of mass destruction, and leaving a stunned music blogger behind to answer for all of it, etc.

Coda

I was taken to a Magneto-esque security facility. A mountain of evidence connected me to Airee's trail of destruction, up to and including my willing participation in said trail of destruction. They considered me beyond dangerous, despite every willing effort I made to comply with them.

I answered every question truthfully. I told them every single thing I could possibly remember about what happened. All about the Ten Charts and the Viereck recordings. All about the portal to the wrong dimension and then the portal to the right dimension. All about the command-and-control language that was woven into each of the tracks that Airee released from her album. Even "Overture," the track without vocals, utilized musical themes of command and control that were diabolical in their effectiveness. I told them all about how Earth was secretly a prison planet for the worst individuals from some hellish future where at least once, Airee had succeeded in erasing some of her enemies from ever having existed. I made it clear that whoever "Airee Macpherson" was on paper, she'd been annihilated long ago by a criminal psychopath from another dimension, who'd taken over her body, and then escaped back to her home on the back of a war beast that she'd summoned down out of the sky. I was very lucid and rational about all of this.

And I was extremely clear: if they cared at all about the future of the planet, they needed to destroy the thumb drive they'd confiscated from me. Under no circumstances could anyone ever be exposed to track ten. They nodded politely.

I was deemed criminally insane. I spent a lot of time in bad places.

. . .

Every now and then, they'd come back and start over with the same questions. Maybe they were trying to catch me in a lie. Maybe scientific advances were catching up to the phenomena they'd observed and they needed my unique perspective. Maybe they were just freakishly bored and I was the only target in the vicinity. I saw the same interrogators over and over again, and I told them the same stories, over and over again.

But I must confess, my aversion to the idea of track ten getting out certainly diminished over time. I might have even suggested, once or twice, that someone should maybe go ahead and listen to it—you know, in a sound-proof room, on a device that could never be connected to the internet, just for the sake of science, you understand. They always nodded politely. I never had any idea what the hell they actually wanted.

. . .

Maybe ten years after I last saw Airee Macpherson, I got an unexpected visitor. They dragged me into a small conference room and chained me to a table and left me alone for an hour, and then the door finally opened, and a young woman in a crisp military uniform came in and sat down across from me. We were silent for a while, eyeing each other.

Then I realized—this wasn't one of my periodic interrogators. This woman had a different look about her. Like she was unnaturally excited to be here. And then my dim-witted eyes finally adjusted, and I realized I was looking at Sierra Nelson. She smiled when I recognized her and said something in a horrible, guttural language that I knew immediately to be the language of the Ten Charts.

"What's going on?" I asked.

"Track ten just got out," she said. "Airee's back—like she promised. She's waiting in a bus outside. Tour starts tonight." She unlocked my handcuffs.

"Can't wait to hear it," I said. "What's it called?"

"It's called 'Your Favorite Band Cannot Save You,'" she said. "C'mon, let's hit the road—it's a long drive to Lawrence."

Acknowledgments

Thanks to Jen Moon and Kira Franz, my beta readers; Lee Harris, my editor; Brady Forrest; Joe and Ola Pemberton; and Ramez Naam.

About the Author

Photograph by Ian Johnston

SCOTTO MOORE is a Seattle playwright whose works include the black comedy *H. P. Lovecraft: Stand-up Comedian!*, the sci-fi adventures *Duel of the Linguist Mages* and *interlace [falling star]*, the gamer-centric romantic comedy *Balconies,* and the a cappella sci-fi musical *Silhouette.* He is the creator of *The Coffee Table,* a comedic web series about a couple who discover their new coffee table is an ancient alien artifact that sends their house shooting through the void (thecoffeetable.tv).

TOR·COM

**Science fiction. Fantasy. The universe.
And related subjects.**

*

More than just a publisher's website, *Tor.com*
is a venue for **original fiction, comics,** and
discussion of the entire field of SF and fantasy,
in all media and from all sources. Visit our site
today — and join the conversation yourself.